The U1
Of Friendship

or
Be What You Are

by

Mark Ellis Brown

The Uncertainties Of Friendship (2nd Edition)
First published 2020 by Kindle Direct Publishing
ISBN: 9798638304096

To Mary

Without whom I might never have known the Island and this story would not be as it is

CONTENTS

Chapter One

Prelude - In Primary School

"Settle down, now settle down everybody please!" called the young teacher from the front of the class. This was her first term in her first teaching post at St Ninian's Junior School, and she was anxious to be accepted by her class of 8 and 9 year olds, but she was after all still finding her feet.

"Well," she said brightly, after calling the register, "I hope you all had a good half-term holiday and I'm sure you're looking forward to Guy Fawkes Night next week. Who's already got their fireworks?" A number of excited hands shot up. "We're going to talk about Guy Fawkes later on this morning in our History period. But right now I need to introduce you all to a new classmate who has just arrived today. Her name is Rowena Brook and she's sitting over there in the corner at the back. Welcome, Rowena!"

Everybody in the class immediately turned round to stare at the newcomer. She was slight and looked skinny and pinched. She had dark hair and dark eyes which flashed out of an angular face.

She sat with shoulders hunched in the classic defensive position of someone clearly nervous and uncertain of her new surroundings. Her lack of confidence was immediately picked up by the unerring antennae of just about the whole class. And she had an unusual, if not a funny, name. Meanwhile, the teacher continued with her introduction.

"Rowena joins us halfway through the term because she has only just moved into the area from another school in a different part of the country. "That's right, isn't it, Rowena?"

Rowena stood up and said: "Yes it is, Miss." She sounded posh to most of the children in the class.

"Oh please, sit down, Rowena. You don't have to stand up to answer questions from a teacher at this school. Is that what you did at your last school?"

Rowena sat down hesitantly, and embarrassed. "Yes, Miss, sorry." Everyone turned and stared at her again. They scented fun. They saw a posh girl looking smart in a clean white shirt and the school tie, setting her apart from the rest of the class. To them she looked quite out of place, unattractive, unconfident. And what about that unfashionable name? She might as well have had a large sign above her screaming "I'm different"; clearly she was going to be a target for any bully boy and spiteful girl in the class. You could sense a wave of glee running round the classroom. Without realising it, the teacher was about to start the ball rolling, to begin Rowena's misery, when she announced:

"On Wednesday, that is, in two days' time, we're going to have a 'Show & Tell' in the class, and I want you all to choose your most recent birthday present, or one of them, to bring into school to show the class and talk about it for just a minute. Nothing longer than that, for those of you who aren't used to Public Speaking." She made it sound very grand. "Nothing to be frightened about, but it will be good for you to have experience of standing up and talking out loud to a lot of people. No, Craig Marshall, you obviously can't bring anything as big as a bicycle! What you all choose must be small enough to be carried in your school bag."

Craig Marshall, a boisterous know-it-all of a boy, turned to his mates and grinned. He considered that his question, as well as being 'witty' as he thought, had scored a point for Team Class vs the Teacher.

What the teacher had *not* stopped to consider was the social make-up of her mixed class, and in particular that the children came from families with very varying levels of income. Those from the lowest income families would most likely have far less significant presents than those from the middle class and higher-income families, where the size or nature of the chosen present might give embarrassment to the child presenting it. And what if the child had unemployed parents and therefore also the possible misfortune not to have received a present at all?

Earlier, the teacher had been told the circumstances surrounding Rowena's sudden appearance at school, but of course none of the class knew, and it would have been inappropriate for her to have told them. As it happened, Rowena's father had only recently lost his job as a local bank manager in Somerset when the branch had been closed by Head Office. He had been relocated to this large town in the Midlands but had to accept a much lower paid position in order to continue working. Worse still for the family, the relocation meant his having been able to buy only a much smaller house in the suburbs for a much higher price than the sale value of their previous house. Consequently, for the time being, the family found themselves existing on Not Very Much; all luxuries were out.

Nevertheless, Wednesday arrived quickly and the class was buzzing with the excitement either of what they had to show off or what they could learn about others through the present being shown. What would the posh girl show? Jokes about 'hockey sticks' and 'tiaras' were already circulating.

When it came to Rowena's turn to stand up and walk out to the front of the class, heads turned eagerly towards her. But she walked up slowly, growing redder in the face with every step. In front of everyone, she stared at the floor and said nothing. She had nothing in her hands. Eventually, she took a deep breath, lifted her head, stared at the class defiantly and said: "I didn't get a proper birthday present this year." She paused, and then said bravely: "My parents weren't able to." Which was the truth, although it didn't explain why, and she definitely wasn't going to tell them.

She walked back to her desk with some girls whispering to each other, some girls openly laughing at her, and boys like Craig Marshall and his mates sniggering loudly. The rest of the boys probably couldn't even bother to react – she was only a *girl* after all. She reached her desk, red as a beetroot and biting her lip. She collapsed on her chair and buried her head in her hands, hating everyone. But she wouldn't cry, she wouldn't let them see how wounded she felt. No new friends here; it felt like being surrounded by hungry jackals.

The teacher carried on around the class. She reached Toby Stannard. He was an average boy who got along with most of his peers, although he tended to steer clear of people like Craig Marshall and Co. But he was also quite a sensitive lad and he had foreseen the inherent flaw in the teacher's 'Show & Tell' plan. And he was quite angry about it. As it happened, his parents had met Rowena's and had mentioned a little of their reduced circumstances to him. So he wasn't surprised at Rowena's revelation. He didn't actually dislike her but then, she wasn't easy to like either. As far as he was concerned, she wasn't fun or friendly and didn't seem to smile much - not that he had anything to do with her. But he felt strongly that no-one deserved to be embarrassed in the way that she had clearly been hurt. He had seen from her face what an effort it had been to her to tell the truth – dangerous information – when it had come to her turn, and he decided he wanted to do something about it.

"Toby," called the teacher. "What have you brought along to show us?"

He stood up but did not walk out to the front of the class. The birthday present he had chosen to bring was beside him in his satchel, but he left it there. Instead, he took a big breath and said, quite clearly: "I didn't get a birthday present either, this year!" He glared around at the class, daring the girls to laugh or Craig and his cronies to snigger at him. The girls in the class didn't care; after all, he was just another "stupid boy". But one or two of his close friends looked at him in surprise, knowing that he hadn't told the truth – luckily for him, none of them spoke up at that point.

"Alright, Toby," said the teacher. "Thank you. You may sit down again." And she continued on to the next person.

Toby sat up straight with his arms folded. He glanced across at Rowena but saw that she was still hiding her head in shame. So he just stared straight ahead until the 'Show & Tell' came to a close.

At break-time, he went to find Rowena who was on her own, trying to look busy with things in her desk.

"That was unfair," he tried saying to her. "Why didn't you lie and say you had something large but your mother wouldn't let you bring it to school, like Miss Buxton told Craig? I know for a fact both Craig Marshall and Paul Haines lied about having big presents when they'd already told some of us that they'd only been given small ones. They were bragging because they were afraid to look silly by telling the truth." He was only trying to be helpful and not hurt her feelings even more. "At least you told the truth. I think that was being jolly brave," he added.

"Oh go away and leave me alone!" She didn't look at him. She was still far too embarrassed and touchy about it, and wasn't ready to be friendly with anyone.

"I don't want to talk to you!" she said angrily, picking up her things and running off. He shrugged and left her to it What did he care about a silly girl anyway? It's not as if he actually *liked* her or anything.

But underneath he knew he did care, not so much about her but rather about the cause of the whole unpleasantness and the injustice of it all. And it bothered him occasionally to the extent that he found himself thinking about it over the next week or two…..

….. and remembered it again at the start of the Spring Term straight after Christmas and the New Year, when Miss Buxton made the same mistake and announced another 'Show & Tell', this time based on a chosen Christmas present. Clearly *some*one hadn't learned the lesson of the previous occasion.

By this time, Rowena had acquired the nickname of "Orphan Annie" which, more unkindly, had soon become shortened to "Orphan". She kept herself to herself as far as she could and hadn't managed to make any proper friends in the class. Some of the girls still teased her if the opportunity arose, or scowled at her for being "posh" if she knew something they didn't. Some of the boys would "tch" loudly if she got a question wrong, whether they themselves knew the right answer or not. She was not popular and knew it, which helped her self-confidence not one bit. And it showed.

The morning of the second 'Show & Tell' arrived and Toby was curious to see if she had something to bring this time. Once again, he found that she hadn't brought anything to show as a Christmas present. Before school started that morning, he had made a point of pretending to bump into her – literally - to check, hoping that there wouldn't be a repeat of the previous term's disaster. He said Sorry for being clumsy, and quickly found a quieter corner where he asked her:

"Remember last time? That was horrid, wasn't it? Look, if you haven't been able to bring something, then you could take the book I've brought in, and pretend it was your Christmas present, if you like. I'll just say I forgot to bring my present and will bring it in tomorrow if Miss Buxton still wants me to – which I bet she won't."

He caught an immediate angry reaction from Rowena. "I don't need *your* help, Toby Stannard!" She turned on her heel and started to march away in indignation. Then, after several steps, she stopped, pausing as if thinking hard. Slowly she turned round and walked back to him as he stood there, still open-mouthed and indignant at the unexpected blast, when he was only trying to be helpful again after all. But the anger had gone from her face.

"Yes, please. I'm sorry I was so rude to you just then. And I wasn't very nice to you the last time either. You were only trying to help, weren't you? Yes, they were all so horrible to me. And unfair. I was so upset. And you stuck up for me, didn't you?" She was still talking in that "posh" way of hers but Toby didn't seem to notice it.

"It would be awfully nice of you if you could lend me your book now, before we go into class," and she gave him an apologetic smile.

"OK, here you are then," he said handing her a copy of Kipling's 'The Jungle Book'. "It's the real thing, you know, the original story. Not like the Disney film, remember it? But as everyone will have seen the film and so think they know all about it already, you probably won't have to say much about the book."

"What can I say about it then, if Miss Buxton asks me?"

"Oh, just say you've only just started to read it and so far it seems very much like the film. Doesn't matter if that's true or not – nobody will care anyway, 'cos you're talking about a *book*. You know, *boring*!"

She thanked him, and went off to Registration on her own. He hung back, reluctant to be seen with her. No point in inviting trouble.

The 'Show & Tell', when it happened later that morning, passed off without incident. There was no repetition of the previous term's embarrassment, and Miss Buxton seemed to accept Toby's excuse quite happily at having "forgotten" to bring in his present. Which Rowena handed back to him privately in the dinner break.

Thankfully, there were no more 'Show & Tell' sessions after that – Miss Buxton had obviously moved onto other more important things. For the rest of that year, Rowena continued to keep herself to herself, and Toby was happy to keep it that way, although they found it easier to tolerate each other from that time. At the end of the summer term, Rowena left to go to a new school – presumably her parents' fortunes had improved by then. But Toby was too busy with his own life to give it, or her, any more thought.

Chapter Two

The Tour – Part 1: Two Girls

Almost twenty years later.

Toby had moved schools at 11 and had been sent to a grammar school away from home where he had to board during term-time. He had kept up with a couple of his best mates at St Ninian's during the holidays, but otherwise his years there were definitely in the past – very quickly nothing more than a memory.

He left his grammar school with a respectable clutch of A-levels, went through college, and subsequently made a career for himself in the world of Publishing. Now 28, he was still unmarried, though he enjoyed platonic friendships with one or two girl friends. He had developed an appreciation of late-medieval church architecture. Coincidentally, and by virtue of his French studies at school and later on, he found himself sent over to France occasionally to his Head Office in Paris which had a regional distribution centre in Rouen. His journeys to Rouen quickly made him aware of the grandeur of the cathedral – another Notre Dame - and the church of Saint-Maclou, and also the monastery of Saint-Ouen. How differently they compared to their English counterparts.

What else might Normandy have to offer of a similar nature? Some simple research answered that question for him – Normandy after all was a significantly large region in its own right and clearly had a whole lot more to offer. So much so that he had determined to take part of his annual leave that year in the form of a road trip to visit some of those places.

The only trouble was that he didn't fancy doing a journey like that on his own. He'd not had a regular girlfriend for quite some time, who might have made an appreciative companion. His 'platonics' either weren't free or else weren't sufficiently keen on the idea. And he certainly didn't have a single pal who would be in the least bit interested in a week of looking round French churches! He'd have to find a group to join – a small-ish one if possible – and just take them on spec. Well, he thought, I managed that a few years ago when I joined that Ramblers Association trip to the Austrian Tyrol, when the rest of the group were all so obviously middle-aged.

So he had taken the unusual step of signing up for a 6-day coach tour around Normandy, in early September after the French national holiday period was over. The tour provided hotel accommodation at the end of each day, with the itinerary including the main churches in places like Amiens, Rouen, Bayeux, Coutances and Chartres, with some other towns as well. The climax of the tour would be a visit to Mont St Michel. The added bonus of the trip was, for him, that he would also get to see plenty of the Normandy countryside, including at least a part of the Cherbourg peninsula. He considered himself a reasonably sociable chap, so a coach tour with other like-minded, interested – and, he hoped, interesting – people could help to make the holiday more enjoyable.

On joining the group, he found a mix of a few middle-aged or retired couples including friends travelling together, and also a number of singles of varying ages – four women and three men including himself. He quickly counted a total of nineteen in the group, which of course would explain why they were all getting on a large minibus and not into a full-sized coach. OK, cosy, he thought, but it looked like a 24-seater, so there should be enough spare seats for any singles who wanted to sit on their own for a bit of privacy. He suspected that the singles would be encouraged to 'couple up' in the bus and swap around each day, if not actually made to do so.

He found he had guessed right. The courier and guide, a pretty 30-something French girl called Anne-Marie, having introduced herself and welcomed everyone on board, immediately laid down that very stipulation to the seven singles – and anyone else who might want to. Anne-Marie had the gift of making an instruction sound like an invitation-without-obligation – she had a delightfully bright voice and her English pronunciation, while being perfectly comprehensible, was nevertheless charmingly French. She playfully "threatened" the singles with a daily rota if she didn't see them mixing in when they got on the bus each morning.

He took stock of his new travelling companions who had taken seats randomly in ones and twos around the bus at the start. His eyes quickly passed over the six couples in order to form a first impression of the six singles. The two gentlemen looked on the elderly side, so were very probably retired – Toby thought they might prove interesting to talk to. Of the ladies on their own, one looked to be in her sixties, and a second at first glance came across as bookish and definitely matched the stereotypical librarian "of uncertain years". The other two were much younger, girls in their twenties, who on closer inspection seemed to know each other already and had perhaps simply arrived separately. Either way, they had palled up immediately and had sat down together.

Given the seating instruction, Toby made a bee-line for the older of the two gentlemen and introduced himself. Go for the one more likely to fall asleep on the way, he thought – clever ruse, until they all had time to get used to each other and become more sociable. Probably take a couple of days, he reckoned; everyone should have got warmed up by the end of Day 3.

Anne-Marie announced that they would be crossing the channel via the Tunnel at lunchtime (which they already knew), and that their first stop in France would be Boulogne, less than half-an-hour's drive down the motorway. There they would visit the Notre Dame Basilica and then have time to stroll around the area and find a café for a drink before continuing on to their overnight hotel at Amiens. She stressed that, unlike many organised tours, this one was not of the whirlwind variety. The itinerary, she said, had been designed to run at a relaxed and comfortable pace with none of the 'early starts' and hectic programmes that most tours seem to demand. "It is your holiday, after all," she told them.

"That's a relief!" Toby commented to his neighbour, elderly James Penridge who was absorbed with the Times crossword. He acknowledged Toby's remark with a polite nod of his head and a half-smile but otherwise made no reply. No early conversation there, thought Toby, and he settled into his seat and got out his book. It was a copy of Kipling's 'Kim' and he was keen to get well into it. Departure time was at 10.00 that morning, but the bus was leaving from central London so it would be some time before they hit the Tunnel and emerged on French soil. Anne-Marie reckoned it would take around three hours to reach Boulogne, given the waiting time at Folkestone.

In due course they reached their first destination, the Notre Dame Basilica, having stopped off earlier at a motorway *Aire* to get a snack lunch. As interesting as the edifice was, with its unusual huge tall dome at the eastern end, Toby had to admit that he was more taken with the scale model reconstruction of the old cathedral as it was around the end of the 16th century, and the information boards about the building's history. He said as much to James over a cup of coffee in a nearby café afterwards, which led to a conversation back on the bus later whereby James gave Toby a potted history of Boulogne and its links with Britain going back to Roman times. Eventually James seemed to run out of steam, and they passed the rest of the journey to the hotel at Amiens in companionable silence.

On arrival at the overnight hotel, Anne-Marie checked the five singles: the three men and the two older ladies, to confirm that they had already paid their single-room supplements for the tour accommodation. At which point, Toby offered to share with either of the other gentlemen if there should be any problem of room allocation in any of the hotels during the trip – and provided of course that a twin-bedded room could be provided! He added that he hoped – for everyone's sake – that this would not be needed!   Since the evening dinner was not included in the tour price, he expected to be dining with the others over several nights at least, so would appreciate being able to decamp to a single occupancy each night.

On the following day, Amiens cathedral proved to be really impressive and this made up for any shortcomings or disappointments that Boulogne might have given rise to on Day 1. The highly colourful and ornate porches of the West Front, the forest of towering buttresses at the East end, the avenue of tall columns flanking and supporting both sides of the lofty nave – all visually stunning and providing plenty to talk about afterwards on the journey to Honfleur, their destination for dinner and the night.

On that drive, Toby was 'obeying orders'; and had changed to sit with the other older gentleman who introduced himself as Ken Churchill "but no relation to the great man" as if he thought his listener would immediately jump to that conclusion. Toby let it pass without comment and put it down to an old man's attempt to help break the ice with something approaching humour. As it turned out, they had an interesting conversation on the delights of Amiens cathedral, both inside and out, and the time to Honfleur passed very quickly. And they also had the graceful Pont de Normandie to admire as they crossed close to the mouth of the Seine towards the end of their journey. He did not get much further with 'Kim'.

In Honfleur that evening, the harbourside restaurants were plentiful and in such attractive surroundings that the whole group wandered down from the hotel to have dinner. Toby and Ken joined two of the couples to make up a table of six, and the whole evening was spent in a convivial atmosphere, especially as one of the other couples and, separately, the two girls had also chosen to eat at the same place. The food was good and the prices very reasonable. After the meal, the evening being still warm and pleasant, they strolled around the whole harbour area before returning to the hotel and bed.

The next morning, it was clear over breakfast that the previous evening had done much to help the group become generally more comfortable – and therefore more sociable – with each other. It was a relatively short journey westwards to Bayeux where the cathedral proved to be, if anything, almost as solid as Amiens but with more open flying buttresses, and altogether no less imposing. This was the morning's event. In the afternoon, there was the obligatory visit to see the Bayeux Tapestry – that is, no-one wanted to miss that chance. And, as an extra bonus, they were taken to their overnight hotel along the coast road of the WW2 Normandy Landings beaches, bound for Arromanches. Here they had the chance to see the remains of Churchill's Mulberry harbours, a few sections still anchored offshore opposite the town, by which the Allied beachhead was supplied from the sea for ten whole months following D-Day back in June 1944. All of which provided plenty of talking points over dinner that evening.

The following day, they were en route to the famous Mont-St-Michel abbey via a stop-off in the town of Coutances as a convenient point for a comfort break together with a short visit to the cathedral there. This was Day 4 and by now Toby felt that he had done enough 'bus-socialising' to have earned himself a seat on his own. He really wanted to get on with 'Kim' without interruptions. He had enjoyed the countryside of the Cherbourg peninsula through which they passed on the way to Coutances, but he hadn't been terribly impressed with the cathedral – not easy when comparing it to Amiens and Bayeux. After the stop, he found there were fewer distractions outside as they travelled towards the Brittany border, and he was able to read far into the book.

There was the inevitable sense of excitement as everyone dismounted from the bus in one of the many car parks on the edge of the Mont-St-Michel complex. For some of the group who had been there before, they were disappointed to find that the causeway leading to the island had been seriously tarmacked over and visitors had to take a bus all the way if they didn't want to walk. As completely impressive as the whole place was, it was unfortunate that one could hardly move for the hordes of tourists of all nationalities thronging into the narrow alleyways at the foot of the abbey. Even Anne-Marie expressed shock at the amount of tourist shops now crammed inside the outer walls. Fighting their way through the dense crowds was so much of a challenge that, by the end of the visit when the group had at last regained the sanctuary of their own bus, everyone pronounced themselves exhausted and ready for the long 2-hour drive to their next overnight stop at the alpine-esque watering hole that was Bagnoles-de-l'Orne. Toby was set on finishing 'Kim'.

The seats directly behind Toby were empty but behind them the two girls were sitting. At one point he had got up to check something with Anne-Marie and, returning to his own seat, he noticed that the girl by the window was evidently trying to sleep, while her friend was looking distinctly bored and restless. A short while later, he heard her change seats and thump down on the seat directly behind him. He carried on reading, but was aware of sounds from behind which showed that the occupant was unable to settle. He had just reached the last chapter when the sound of someone getting up was immediately followed by a body planting itself in the seat right next to him. It was the same girl.

"Hi, I'm Claudia," she said with gusto, "but you can call me Claude – everyone does." She spoke with a slight accent that would have been called "well-bred" rather than actually "posh".

"Oh, hi, I'm Toby" he returned, in some surprise, and a little irritated at the interruption. He shook the limp hand she held out. Ah well, he thought, better make conversation. "How are you and your friend enjoying the trip? With such a small group, it's a bit weird that we haven't found ourselves being introduced before now."

"No, the tour's going OK – I'm enjoying it. It's a good pace – nothing too energetic! I think the hotels are a bit basic, though. But then, they are only 3-star, aren't they? Still, it's only for five nights so I reckon we can put up with it."

"It could be worse," replied Toby in as non-committal a way as he could without actually being rude. It was clear that she was going to do all the talking, but also that he couldn't very well return to finish the final chapter without risking giving offence. He sighed and settled back to listen.

"No, it was such a fantastic coincidence. You know, that Fran and I were having a drink the other day a few weeks ago and found that we were about to book ourselves onto the same tour!" She indicated the sleeping girl two rows back. "We've known each other on and off for several years, I mean, we've done the occasional thing together. She's OK, if a little inclined to give herself airs sometimes, if you know what I mean. Anyway, we agreed that we could share a room together and so naturally we've been going around together since we started. But you need a change from time to time, don't you? Can't sit with the same person all the time, can you? So here I am!"

As tired as he felt, Toby was beginning to feel exhausted just listening to the insistent breeziness of The Interruption. He tried not to show it but it was difficult. Was she always like this? He grunted some sort of assent to the last remark, to show that he had heard. She carried on regardless, talking about all the things they had seen so far, and the travelling in between places, and the food, and the hotel rooms. She seemed to be able to move seamlessly from one topic to the next with hardly a pause. Toby knew she meant well, and also that she needed some way of relieving her boredom. He just wished she hadn't chosen him at that particular point of the day.

Just when he thought she'd run out of finding new things to say, she leant over and said: "Oh, what are you reading? I can see you've nearly finished it!"

He showed her the Kipling.

"Never read it myself" she said. "Didn't he write 'The Jungle Book'?"

"Well, 'Jungle Books' actually. He wrote two of them," replied Toby. "But he wrote stacks of other stuff as well, including a lot of poems. I like him very much although I believe he's gone right out of fashion now. His style is condemned for being associated too strongly with Edwardian imperialism. You can see why, though I also think it's a bit unfair. People always find it easier to criticise than to make the effort to understand."

Claudia held up her hands in mock protest.

"Hey, don't look at me," she said. "What do I know? History was never my strong point, though of course I'm against slavery and exploitation and all that sort of thing. You need to talk to Fran about that – she's the one interested in history and she's got opinions that you may, or may not, agree with. Say," she said, changing the subject rapidly. "What do you think about Chartres where we're going tomorrow? Ever been there? I haven't. Heard it should be spectacular, though."

And on she went. And on. In the end, Toby switched to auto-pilot, and let his mind wander away. Claudia didn't seem to notice. And when they reached Bagnoles and were coming down into the town, she got excited about the lake and the alpine feel to some of the architecture. Toby had enough nous to come back to reality and the moment, and to thank her politely for her company as she switched seats back to her friend, to wake her up and show her the new sights. He'd finish 'Kim' in his room later that evening, after dinner.

He'd retired to his room as soon as he decently could after the meal. It was as he was finally finishing the book that there was a tentative knock on his door. He found it was the other girl, Fran, who was standing there, dark hair loose about her shoulders.

"Sorry to bother you so late. It's Toby, isn't it? Claude told me. By the way, I'm Frances, definitely not 'Fran' – I wasn't actually asleep on the bus while she was in full spate next to you," she said pointedly. "And I don't like 'Frankie' or 'Fanny' either. she added. "Especially not the last one!"

"Hi, Frances," replied Toby. "No, I don't care for the others either, so I think we're OK."

"Look," said Frances. "Sorry it's a bit cheeky but I really need a second pillow before I can get to sleep, and I wondered if you might have one you could spare from your room? They've only given us one each, and I can't be doing with those French bolsters. Claude thought you might be able to help – we're just a couple of doors down from you."

"Come on in a moment," said Toby. "I'll have a quick look round." It was soon apparent that there was no spare pillow in his room either, and he wasn't sure if the concierge could be found that late to search one out for her. "Sorry," he told her. "Obviously I need mine. But will this do, just for one night?" He rummaged in his bag and produced a blow-up travel pillow. "I take it everywhere with me for just such an emergency. It's proved very useful. Would you like to try it? You can return it to me in the morning on the bus."

"Thanks," she said gratefully. "I'll have a go. It's got to be better than not."

"So put it under your proper pillow. And you may need to put a folded-up towel there as well, to make it more like the same width as your real pillow. That way, hopefully your head won't slide off while you're asleep."

She asked him: "Will you be alright with the bolster for one night? It's awfully kind of you."

"I don't like them either, but it's OK – I can manage" he replied gallantly.

She thanked him again and left.

Chapter Three

The Tour – Part 2: Frances

The next morning was going to be taken up with a long 3-hour drive across to Chartres. Toby was one of the first on the bus and chose a window seat. Some of the couples followed, and then the two girls got on and, as before, went to sit two rows behind him. The bus was starting off when Frances, remembering, rummaged in her bag and produced Toby's inflatable pillow. She came over and sat down beside him. He noticed that her long dark hair was tidier than it had been the previous evening, held in place by a smart red woollen cap. Possibly some sort of slightly eccentric fashion statement? he wondered idly.

"OK. Here you are. Returned as promised. Thanks very much – you came to my rescue there. I would have had a bad night without it."

"How did it work out? Did you keep slipping off the pillow?" asked Toby.

"Surprisingly, no" replied Frances. "Thanks for the tip about using a folded towel as well – I think that's what did the trick." She settled back into the seat and showed no immediate intention of going back to sit with Claudia. "Mind if I sit here with you for a bit? Claude tells me you're a bit of a Kipling fan and I should check that you're not after all an imperialist lackey! Whatever she means by that!"

"Oh, I get it. I just stuck up for what he wrote about and the way he wrote. I guess these days you just either love him or hate him. Each to his own, as they say."

"So what do you do?" she asked directly. Toby thought she had a gentle and quite attractive voice - at least, nothing like Claudia's wearying breeziness of the day before.

"Oh, I work for a French publishing house, at their London offices near Southwark cathedral. I did Business French at college so I get sent over to France on business occasionally, which I guess is how I got interested in doing a trip like this. How about you?"

"That's a coincidence! I work near there for Lloyds in their foreign currency dept – er, trading, you know."

"Sounds interesting. And a bit high-powered? It must be fascinating seeing how much arbitrage goes on!"

At this, she surprised Toby by looking blankly at

him, as if she had no idea what he was talking about. But she'd said she worked in Forex trading, hadn't she?

"Well, at least you must work with stacks of world currencies," he went on, trying to avoid a potential embarrassment.

"Oh yes," she said brightly. "It's not all just dollars and euros!"

Which could mean anything or nothing, he thought. Maybe he'd better change the subject quickly. "Do you often go abroad for your holidays? Any exotic places?"

"I went on safari once to the Serengeti with my parents. That was amazing! The tigers especially were brilliant, I remember!"

Hold on, Toby thought. That's not right. Everyone knows there are no tigers in Africa. Should he mention it? It didn't sound like a slip of the tongue somehow.

"Er, you must mean "lions" in the Serengeti?"

"Yes, of course. Yes, that's what I meant. Of course."

"Sorry, didn't mean to embarrass you," Toby said quickly. "Of course you meant 'lions'. I've never been there myself. I must admit I've never found the idea of a safari as compelling as most people seem to. Probably feel differently if I had actually been on one. Now India," he continued, "*there's a place I'd really like to go to if I ever had the money! The Taj Mahal, obviously. And the Golden Temple at Amritsar too. That's close to the border where they have that guard-stamping ceremony every night, trying to outdo the Pakistanis on the other side. I've seen it on TV lots of times."

"Oh, India!" said Frances. I've been there too, thanks to a banking colleague my father knows in Delhi, luckily for me. The Taj was spectacular, breath-taking! And we stayed in a really nice hotel, in Jaipur it was, you know, for seeing the Taj."

What? There she goes again, thought Toby who knew enough about the chief tourist destinations in India to know that the Taj Mahal is at Agra, not Jaipur. I suppose she *could* have made a genuine mistake, he conceded, but it doesn't seem very likely. He decided to say nothing this time. But, he said to himself, it's beginning to sound like she's desperate to impress me for some unknown reason. She doesn't even know me; it doesn't make sense.

"A place I *have* been to," he said, "is Boston in the

States. There's all that history with the famous Boston Tea Party when they were objecting to what they thought was unfair taxation and threw the tea into the harbour! And then there was the equally famous Battle of Bunker Hill during the American War of Independence – there's a memorial obelisk there now."

"Yes, I remember all that stuff from school. And I went there too. Bunker Hill, I mean. The Hill's outside Boston, isn't it? You get a great view from the top – you can see for miles around, can't you?"

Oh-ho, thought Toby. No, you didn't go there. You've never been there, have you? Bunker Hill's not exactly "outside" Boston, being only in the Charlestown suburb. And it's a pretty low hill and there are definitely *no* "views for miles" from the top of it! So what's she up to? It's almost as if she has to top, or at least to equal, anywhere exotic I say I've been to or want to see. As if she needs to show that she's just as good or just as fortunate as everyone else she meets. What did Claudia say yesterday about her: that she "tends to give herself airs"? But she seems normal enough on the surface.

So he made another of his non-committal grunts

as if in agreement. Better steer the conversation away from places abroad. "So what made you choose a tour like this, Frances?"

"Well, I had a week's leave and thought I'd like to see a bit of France. Normandy appealed, partly because it's the closest to home so you don't have to travel for hours just to start, and partly I suppose from the historical point of view. You know, the Hundred Years War: Crécy, Harfleur and Agincourt, Joan of Arc and Rouen. All that. Romantic I know, but being able to include lots of major places in a short space of time seemed a good way to spend what holiday money I had. Then I met up with Claude, told her what I planned, and she said: Why not go together? So we did. And to tell you the truth, I couldn't afford an expensive holiday."

"Who can?" agreed Toby warmly. At last, some honesty coming through; that was a relief. Once again he tried a change of tack with her. "So what was Claude on about yesterday when she said that you "had opinions that I might, or might not, agree with"? It's clear you're into History but what was all that about? It's not as if she knows me well enough to be able to say anything like that with confidence."

"Oh, I don't think she meant much by it. She may

come across as being a bit Old School and she does tend to go with whatever's the flavour of the month in her attitude to things. Like the current attitude towards British imperialism: you know, everyone has to apologise nowadays for historical circumstances beyond their control. I dared to offer a different view – a bit strongly, I'm afraid – about how things being taken out of context make a dubious platform on which to base an argument. Anyway, serves you right for trying to read Kipling in front of her!" she grinned, showing a nice sense of humour. "Sure you're not going to produce any inflammatory reading material this morning?" Laughing this time.

You know, you can be almost charming sometimes, thought Toby. "No, not today. It took me so long to actually finish the last one that I decided to give myself a break from it today. Which is OK because here you are and we're chatting quite happily, and so I can't fall foul of our dear Tourmeister's edict about singles mixing. By which I mean, you're welcome to stay and chat some more if you're not already bored out of your socks and want to return to your other seat. Give it another half-hour and we should get our box ticked by Anne-Marie! I hear she might dish out 'Job Done' stickers at the end of the tour to any singles who have toed the party line!"

Frances looked at him questioningly.

"You know, Scouts and Guides years ago?" He grinned at her. "Sorry, only joking. No such things anymore. And maybe you were never a Guide or a Brownie anyway?"

"It's OK. I got it," she replied. "I sometimes use that phrase myself when I want to be sardonic. Anyway, thanks for the invitation, and I don't mind if I do. For a while at least." She settled back. "So how well do you know France?" she asked him.

"Hardly. I mean, this is as far south as I've ever been. Mind you, I'm thinking of trying a bit further south-west sometime, maybe for a proper holiday one year. September, you know, would be a good time since it's when all the French families have left the coast because the schools start back on the 1st. I'm wondering whether it might be a nice trip to drive down from Calais to somewhere a little further south than the famously windy Vendée. There are a couple of islands off the coast down around La Rochelle, which might be worth considering. I like the sea, but the Med. and Provence are really too far to drive, particularly if you have only a week's leave instead of the typical fortnight. Have you ever hankered after going further than just Normandy?"

"Well, I've wondered about the Dordogne – you know, more of the Hundred Years War thing. Everyone seems to rave about it and tell you just how many English live down there now. Not that that itself is any attraction," she added hastily. "But, you know, time and funds."

"Yes, I do know what you mean." But Toby was actually thinking: if she's in Forex trading, wouldn't she be creaming it? Surely there aren't any poorly paid people in that business? He thought he might venture a question. "The time thing I can understand; they must work you all hours if you're in currency trading. But surely they can't be underpaying you in that line of work? Not that I'm prying, you understand. It just seems a bit odd, that's all."

"Oh, that's easy to answer," returned Frances. "I only started recently so I'm still on my probationary period."

"Yes, of course. That does make sense," replied Toby. "Let's change the subject."

Which they did, and carried on chatting quite comfortably until, at one point, Frances realised that they had been together for the best part of two hours and she felt she ought to get back to

Claudia. "I can't have her thinking I've deserted her for a new boyfriend! See you later." And with that she left him alone again.

He heard her sitting down next to Claudia again with Claudia saying: "Hello stranger! I thought I'd lost you forever. How's Toby? Any sign of wedding bells yet?"

He heard Frances' snorted response of: "Don't be daft! Oh, Toby? He's OK."

He didn't know whether this was a reference to his well-being or to the question whether she liked him or not. Not fussed, either way, he said to himself, and moved up a few rows to sit with Ken.

In due course they reached Chartres. Parking for the cathedral was several streets away so they had a short distance to walk. Toby found himself close behind Frances as they were crossing a main street. He noticed that Frances was more occupied by her surroundings than watching the road as they crossed. Just in time he spotted the cyclist coming from the left and pulled her back as the bike swerved round her to avoid a collision, the cyclist calling out angrily at her as he passed.

"Sorry for jerking you back like that," he said.

"Mad cyclist! I had to act rather quickly. You do just need to remember about traffic coming from the left each time, though."

She was more surprised than shocked – after all, no-one likes to be yanked backwards unceremoniously without any warning at all! But she recovered quickly and thanked him well enough, before hurrying on to rejoin Claudia up ahead.

Outside the cathedral, as usual, Anne-Marie gave them a summary of the building's history. They all agreed it made for a stupendous sight. She pointed out the asymmetric spires at the west end, not that you could miss them, and then walked everyone round to see the magnificent triple porticos on both the north and south transepts. There were more flying buttresses to marvel at. She showed them the large and unusual 24-hour clock on the north side, which reminded Toby of the external clock in a similar place on Wells cathedral.

Inside, the brilliant stained glass held everyone's attention immediately, until she dragged them away to show them the pavement area designed as a labyrinth in the middle of the nave floor. Looking upwards, the vaulted ceiling and the height of the whole nave took a while to take in. The group were then given a good amount of time to wander at will, and she recommended a walk around the cathedral on the east side and down the hill to the streets below.

At the appointed time, everyone gathered at the west front to return to the bus. As they were starting back, Toby noticed that Frances was missing. He checked with Claudia who said she had been with her "only a minute ago". He told Anne-Marie that he would nip back into the cathedral just to see if she had gone back in for a final look. Claudia followed. They soon found her staring fixedly up at the superb Rose window on the north side. This time he touched her gently on the shoulder and, taking her elbow, said quietly: "Come on, we've got to go now. They're waiting for us." Reluctantly she turned towards him and nodded with regret in her eyes. He waved to Anne-Marie as they emerged from the cathedral into the sunlight, and they followed the tail-end of the party back to the bus.

The journey onwards to their overnight stop at Dreux was short and uneventful. The splendour of Chartres cathedral was obviously the main topic of conversation over dinner that evening. And there was a certain amount of relief that there would be no more long 3-hour drives to suffer since they were now less than two hours away from Rouen. After dinner, Frances came and found Toby again.

"Thanks for helping me out the other night. Look, sorry, but can I ask another favour? I need to recharge my camera before Rouen tomorrow and I forgot that I'd need a USB adaptor for the wire. Have you got one you can lend me overnight? And would you also have a French 2-pin adaptor for the English plug? Please?"

"Looks like you're in luck again! I charged mine last night ready for Chartres so I reckon I'll have more than enough battery for Rouen too. So, yes, you can borrow my adaptors. Do you want to come up and get them now?"

"Yes please. Then I can put it on charge straight away. They can sometimes take at least a couple of hours to finish. At least my camera does."

"Same here, although I always carry a small camera as well, as a back-up, just in case. So either way I'm covered. You can let me have the adaptors back tomorrow morning on the bus. OK?"

"Yes, brilliant. Thanks." And off she went.

Once again, the next morning, Toby was already on the bus when the two girls got on. And once again Frances had a quick word with Claudia and came to sit beside him.

"Here are your electrics back, thanks" and she handed over his two adaptors which he stowed away in his cabin bag.

"Do you want to see my pictures of Chartres from yesterday?" she asked.

He was interested to see if she was the sort of photographer to recognise and take unusual angles and to produce shots which were different from the norm, so he said: "Yes, sure." They settled a bit closer to each other so that they could page through the pictures together. He was pleased to see that she had quite an artistic eye and wasn't showing him just run-of-the-mill stuff. He said so, and she smiled nicely at him for the compliment.

She was putting the camera away when the thing happened. Neither knew what caused it but suddenly the camera, which was in her hands one minute, was the next second on the floor, landing heavily on the shutter. Which then refused to open properly when she tested it.

"Oh no! Oh hell! What am I going to do now?" she cried. "I was so looking forward to Rouen, and it's our last stop too."

"Hang on," said Toby. "Check if the card is still OK – it ought to be."

She checked, and with some relief, saw that it

was intact.

"How long have you had it? Any chance that it might still be under warranty?" he asked.

"Well, I haven't had it a whole year yet so, yes, I guess it must still be," she replied.

"Would your warranty cover accidental damage? Then you could send it off to be repaired under warranty when you get home, couldn't you? And meanwhile, if you don't mind making do with a lesser camera, you can use my back-up one." He rummaged in his bag and brought out a small pouch. He showed her the camera inside. "It's a Canon, so it's not all that bad. It's digital OK and runs on two AA batteries, and look, there are a couple of spares in the pouch. You can borrow it for Rouen if you like. It'd tide you over. What do you think?"

Oh. Well …." She sounded doubtful. "I don't know. What about any pictures I take on it?"

"Simple," said Toby. "When I get home, I'll put all your shots onto a disk or a small flash drive and, if you can give me a contact for getting hold of you, I could tell you when it's OK. Maybe we could meet up somewhere in town and I can hand them over. You said you didn't work that far from me in the Southwark area."

At that she brightened up considerably.

"Well, if you're sure? If you really don't mind? That would be a real help. And very kind of you. Again." she added. "That makes three times already this trip. *And* you came back to get me yesterday. You're turning out to be quite a good friend."

"Hey, don't mention it. Glad to be able to help when it's needed," he replied, a little embarrassed. There was a pause during which neither spoke. Then he said, by way of conversation, and in the tone of a teacher:

"So what book have you brought along this morning to share with the class?"

"Oh." She saw that he was making a joke. She put on a suitably mock-apologetic voice. "I'm so sorry, Sir, I forgot to bring it. It's still in my suitcase. It won't happen again, Sir." He grinned at her. She returned to her normal voice. "And what's *your* book this morning? Another Kipling possibly?"

He saw that she wasn't making fun of him, so reached into his bag and brought out his old and well-worn copy of 'The Jungle Book' which he showed her. She inspected the cover. "You've had this for a long time, haven't you?" She opened the fly leaf to see the words 'Happy Christmas, with love from Grannie'. She also read the name: Toby Stannard. She gave a start of surprise. She said, slowly with a hint of suspicion: "I once knew a boy called Toby who had a copy of this book."

"Coincidence?" replied Toby. "It's always been an incredibly popular book. There must be lots of Tobys in the world. Could have been anyone." He paused. "Come to think of it, I once lent this particular copy to a girl in my class at Primary School, to help her out of some sort of bother she was having. What was her name, now?" He screwed his eyes up trying to remember far back in his memory. "I remember her first name was Rowena but I can't for the life of me remember her surname. Not that it matters."

"It might," she said cryptically. She looked at him in a strange way for several moments. "You don't look anything like the boy I remember," she said, which meant nothing to him at all. "Where was your Primary School?"

"Oh, up in the Midlands."

"And the name of your school?"

"Er, it was called St Ninian's Junior. Odd name

really."

She then did something which caused a surprise to them both. She reached into her bag, drew out her purse, and took out her credit card. "Read the name on that," she said.

He read: 'Rowena Frances Brook'. He looked at her, startled. So Frances was her *second* name.

"You're that boy, aren't you!" she said, almost accusingly. "It's the same book, the actual same book, I know it is!"

"So, if it's you, what was the teacher's name?" challenged Toby.

"Miss - er – Miss Buxton, it was. Yes, that's it. I arrived halfway through that first term. I only stayed for a year."

"Wow!" breathed Toby. "It really *is* you! Fancy that! Meeting up again quite by chance after all these years."

"Yes. I remember being angry and quite horrid to you when you were only trying to be kind. If I didn't say Sorry and Thank You properly back then, then take it from me now. And you're *still* being nice to me, and kind. Do I deserve it? How do you manage it? Have you always been like that?"

"On and off over the years, I guess," he said modestly. "Just part of my natural charm." He grinned. "Still, if this book helped you all those years ago, then I'm glad."

"No, *you* helped me, not the book. But I have to admit I never read any Kipling as a result. You'll have to tell me about it sometime."

"Well, if you're serious, I suppose I *could* lend it to you again, if you were very, very careful with it and promised faithfully to return it. It means a great deal to me. You've seen the inscription in it. It makes me think of my grandmother more than anything else I've got. She rarely gave us a present we'd put on our Christmas List unless she thought it was 'worthy'. So that particular year, and since I was doing so well at Cubs at the time, she ignored my List and gave me that book. I've treasured it ever since."

"I think I understand," said the Frances/Rowena. "I had an uncle a bit like that when I was about that age."

"Did you really?" asked Toby, thinking: was she doing it again, this copying for the sake of seeming to be on an equal footing?

"Yes, I did, really" she said in slightly faraway tones, as if remembering a loved relative from the past. "He was Uncle Will, a cousin of my father's, so I suppose technically he wasn't an actual 'uncle' in the normal sense of the word. But he was a direct blood relative on my parents' level so he was a real uncle as far as I was concerned. He could be a bit stiff with you, but he was always fair. And he was always kind. I loved him for it."

"Yes, I do understand that," answered Toby, and immediately he thought better of her. "And, you know, I'm glad I got angry for your sake that day and tried to stand up for you. I think you've turned out OK, anyway." He suddenly felt awkward. "Sorry, no offence. I didn't mean that to sound patronising."

"It's alright," she replied. "No offence taken. In fact, I think it's rather nice to meet someone later in adult life who did you a good turn when they were small. Smaller," she corrected herself.

"Anyway," continued Toby, "if you did want to borrow this 'priceless tome', you could take it home with you and, if you promise to read it sooner and not put it on one side for later, then you could give it me back in exchange for the copy of your Rouen photos, if or when we met up later."

"Thank you," she said. "That's sounds like a good plan." She took both camera and book from him and, in return, wrote her name and mobile phone number on a piece of torn-off note paper which he stowed away in his wallet.

"Phew!" said Toby after a pause. "Well, well, that was a turn-up for the books, and no mistake! So how have you been, since then?"

"Oh, OK. You know, some and some. But mostly 'Some', I guess." She grinned. "Did you know why we'd fallen on temporarily hard times that particular year? Why I came to your school at the half-term?"

"My parents had met yours, I think, and they'd told me maybe the bare minimum, about your father having to change to a less well-paid job after a good one a long way away."

"It took a year for my father's prospects to improve to the point where they could send me to the sort of school they preferred."

"Wasn't it a posh girls' school?"

"Not particularly posh, actually," she said. "But I came to realise later that it did have that sort of reputation. No, it was an OK place, although it took me quite a while to find my feet, and several of the girls looked down on me when they found out I had come from a State school. That lasted for some time, but I got through it, and had no more trouble like that once I got to the 5th Form. Anyway, I came out with a respectable quota of Os and As."

"And after?"

"Had a Gap Year. Wondered what to do with my life, what direction to take. No clear idea. Didn't make university in the end but went through college. Had several jobs in different areas and finally ended up at Lloyds in Southwark. How about you?"

"As I said before, I'm in publishing. Grammar school followed by college. Like you, I didn't make university. I still think I'd quite like to go, but maybe I'm too far past that stage of my life and, anyway, I didn't really like the idea of having to do two subjects. I'd much prefer to be able to concentrate fully on just the one."

"And what would that 'one' have been?"

"Ah well, you see, I could never really decide between History or the Classics or Linguistics. I probably would have fallen between all three stools!" he added ruefully.

"So what do you read for pleasure these days?"

"What? Apart from Tolkien? No, don't look like that, I'm serious! So, yes, I guess I read historical fiction and non-fiction, from the classical period up to early Georgian times. But the fiction has to give me historical fact and background – I don't go for all this fanciful romantic invention. You know what I mean?"

"Yes," she agreed. "You need a bit of substance. The 'Mills & Boon' genre is all very well, and obviously works fine for its readers. But I agree with you that fact is better than speculative invention of the 'behind-the-scenes' variety."

"Hey, we're getting a bit serious and erudite here! Time to change the subject onto lighter things again?" said Toby. "Or do you think you ought to be getting back to Claude now?"

"We seem to have been going for ages. Can't be all that far to go now before we get to Rouen. I guess I'll be sitting with her all the way back to Calais later after we've done Rouen. I might as well stick here until we get there. If you don't mind, that is?"

"Please, be my guest. It's been nice talking to you. I've enjoyed it – not to mention that amazing coincidence! No, you just please yourself. Stay if you'd like or go back if you'd prefer."

"I'm comfortable here," she said simply. And stayed until they all got out of the bus in the centre of Rouen, at which point she rejoined Claudia who forbore this time to mention anything about 'wedding bells' but still looked askance at her friend, implying that she wondered what, if anything, was "going on" between her and Toby.

Once again Anne-Marie herded them all together and announced that they would have plenty of time to visit both the cathedral of Notre Dame in the afternoon and also the nearby church of Saint-Maclou where they would go first. But, given that they would need to get lunch in the city, she regretted that there would not be time on this trip to make a proper excursion into the monastery of Saint-Ouen as well, although she promised that the coach would drive past it so that they could take pictures if they wanted. They would be getting on the motorway towards the end of the afternoon ahead of the rush hour, and have a straight 2-hour drive back to Calais and the Channel Tunnel.

The church of Saint-Maclou was on the small side but intricately decorative in style and a perfect contrast to the magnificence of the cathedrals previously visited on the trip. And it was in a charming part of the town where the buildings were equally photogenic. Indeed, they saw quite a few street artists painting the houses and street scenes in preference to the church itself.

After lunch, the party made their way to the cathedral. Once again, they found it a truly impressive and attractive building. After Chartres on the previous day, everyone was well used to the soaring columns and high vaulted ceiling of the nave but it was a landmark edifice after all and, everyone agreed, a fitting end to the tour.

Afterwards, Frances' inclination to inattention in the street struck again, and once again Toby happened to be on hand to help. He saw straightaway that the traffic around the cathedral was far busier than in Chartres, and the truth was that he decided to contrive to walk just behind her, while as unobtrusively as possible. If it had happened once, he reasoned, it was quite likely to happen again; if so, this time she might not be so lucky.

And, sure enough, it occurred as they were walking back from the cathedral. And this time, as he had feared, it was a car coming fast from her left, as she instinctively looked to her right first before crossing the road. Spotting the danger before it struck, as at Chartres, he had only about a second to react. He grabbed her with both hands and pulled her backwards off the kerb.

For several moments they just stood there, his arms clasping her tightly to his chest as if he feared that another car would actually hit her if he let go. They looked to any idle observer like two lovers, him cuddling her as she gazed across the road. In reality she was suffering a mild attack of shock as a result of realising the crisis that had just been avoided. Toby was simply holding her safely, until she was ready to move on.

Claudia and those nearest crowded around her solicitously. Anne-Marie came hurrying back to check that no disaster had taken place and that Frances was sufficiently recovered to continue. Toby was quick to let her go then and to stand back while others cared for her. It was after all a bit embarrassing, he felt. Twice in two days. What's she on? he wondered.

After about five more minutes, the sense of shock seemed to have passed, and Claudia led Frances away and back to the coach. As she had told Toby previously, Frances sat with Claudia for the whole journey back to Calais, the Tunnel, and on to London. Back at the terminus, as the group were splitting up, saying their farewells and going their separate ways, Frances found Toby to thank him for his prompt action after Rouen cathedral. And for the other ways in which he had helped her during the tour.

"Don't mention it," he said. "It's OK, really it is. Glad to help a fellow classmate – even from yonks ago!" he added with a grin.

"Here's your spare camera back, returned with my thanks," she relied cheerfully. "Now you will remember to contact me as soon as you've got the photos ready for me?"

"Sure," he replied. "Just so long as you don't get a new mobile with a different phone number – and you've given me the right one now, of course! If you've got time, can I just check?" And he fished out the note she had given him earlier.

She checked it for him.

"Yes, that's all fine. At least I can get *some*thing right!," she said.

And then:

"Look, Claude's calling so I'd better go. Well, goodbye. I think it went pretty well overall, and I'm glad I met you again after so many years. It was OK, wasn't it?" And with that, she shook his hand and hurried off over to where Claudia was waving and tapping her watch meaningfully.

Chapter Four

The Dinner

It took Toby only a short while, once he got home, to transfer Frances' photos onto a disk. But he delayed phoning her for nearly a fortnight afterwards, partly to give her time to read the Kipling, and partly because he didn't want to come across as somehow too keen and anxious to stay in touch. I mean, he told himself, she was OK, and quite pleasant company on the whole. Not bad looking actually, nice figure, pretty reasonable in fact, although not what you'd call in any way stunning either. No, he admitted to himself, he wasn't really into 'stunning', not his type: that was just typical male fantasy. Silly – impractical even. Strange in a way that there was nothing he could see of the girl he remembered from Primary School although, to be fair, that particular memory was pretty hazy after so long. At least it was nice that she wasn't skinny any more, he reflected.

So, alright, she was worth at least a date for maybe going out for a meal – you never know how things might turn out. Or it could just as easily prove to be a one-off after which they'd shake hands and go their separate ways. She had a nice smile, he remembered from the coach, which can tell you a lot about a person. But there was also that business about telling evident fibs about her life – he didn't want to use the word 'lies' which didn't feel quite accurate somehow. True, it was a form of dishonesty but there was clearly no malevolent intent in her, so she was only kidding herself, wasn't she? If he was going to see her again, albeit probably once only, he'd perhaps better give it some more thought. Just what was it all about?

His first two calls to her mobile reached her voice-mail. He left his number but she didn't call back. So he sent her a text and then phoned again the following day. This time she answered. No apology for not getting back to him earlier, but he didn't bother about it. He remembered to check with her that she had access to a laptop or desktop for reading the photos off the disk.

They agreed on a place for food, and a meeting time on the following Wednesday evening, for exchange of disk and book over an Italian. Keep it simple, Toby thought. Nothing flash. No risk of possible wrong signals. Nevertheless, on the day itself, he found himself quite looking forward to seeing her again that evening. He rather liked the prospect of trying to find out a bit more about her and what was making her tick in that particular way.

As courtesy dictated, he arrived at the Italian restaurant slightly ahead of schedule. He was pleased that she showed up less than ten minutes late – so hardly 'late' at all – and had obviously been hurrying to get there. She apologised immediately, and he made the customary "Not at all. Don't mention it" reply. He saw she was wearing the same little red woollen cap she had worn in France.

They were shown to a table and quickly ordered drinks before turning to study the menu, each one feeling a little self-conscious. Only when they had given their order to the waiter did they begin to relax and the latent tension between them start to disappear. Toby opened the bidding.

"It's nice to see you again. I'm glad you were able to make it." She smiled her acknowledgment. "Here's the disk. You'll see on it that I added just one or two of my own photos which I thought might complement the ones you took in Rouen. You can ignore or delete them as you wish."

"OK. Thanks for doing that for me, and lending me the camera in the first place, of course. I've only just got mine back from being repaired. Oh, and here's your 'Jungle Book'; I've taken great care with it." She laughed. "And that's the second time in my life I've done that now."

"The pleasure's all mine" replied Toby in mock gallantry. "No, really, how did you get on with it? You don't have to like it, of course, but I'd be interested to know what you thought."

"Er, well," she began, "I'm going to confess that I didn't read the whole book. I obviously read all the stories directly about Mowgli, with Shere Khan out to kill him all the time, and where he returns to a village but can't adjust to the structured life of the humans. And of course there's the famous separate story about Rikki-Tikki Tavi and his war against the cobras. So I can appreciate how the book is regarded as a classic, and how there is an appeal to the way Kipling writes. But don't you think it's a bit 'Boys Own'? You know, the independent go-where-you-like maverick boy stereotype?"

"I'm not sure I would describe Mowgli as a stereotype – quite the reverse, in fact," answered Toby. "But I think I see what you mean."

"One thing I did appreciate," she said, "was the key at the back of your edition which told you the authentic pronunciation of the characters' names. You do wonder on first reading. Something that Walt Disney didn't bother to research, clearly!"

Toby nodded in agreement. And then thought it was time to change the subject. He wanted to find out a bit more about her past. Already knowing the answer, because Claudia had told him back on the tour, he asked Frances:

"So have you known Claudia long? I couldn't help wondering if you met each other at the school you went to after you left St Ninian's. Of course, I may be completely wrong – and you can shoot me down if I am – but somehow you gave me the impression that you'd gone on to an independent girls' school, maybe even a boarding school. Am I anywhere near the mark?"

"OK, Sherlock, you guessed right. What gave me away, Inspector?"

"Ah now, the criminal mind always makes one fatal mistake!" he said, giving a parody of the typical master-sleuth. "No, but Claudia?"

"We knew each other in the 6th Form although she was in the year above me so we didn't actually go around together. We happened to meet up again later in London, several years into our careers."

"Ah yes, your career" he ventured. "You said you work for Lloyds in foreign currencies. Trading, wasn't it?"

"Er, well ......" she began, sheepishly and suddenly not so sure of herself. He jumped in, eager to save her from any immediate embarrassment.

"I only ask, because – and I know this is probably far too below what you do – well, I've got a load of Amex travellers cheques left over from that Boston trip I did, and I want to cash them. I thought you might be able to advise me."

He was somewhat surprised how full her advice was as she gave him chapter and verse about the procedure for encashment and even the back office procedure by which the bank recovered its funds from Amex.

"Wow! Thanks," he said. "I never dreamt there was so much to it! You really know your stuff."

"Oh well, you know ....." she said, leaving her sentence unfinished.

"Ah, thank you," they said to the waiter who had just brought their starter.

Toby went on: "I bet you never thought, back there in Primary School that you would end up in such a high-powered job."

Again she was reticent in her reply.

"Oh, not really high-powered. Not as such, anyway."

There was an awkward pause.

"Look" she said. "I rooted out this old class photo which they took that year when we were both there at St Ninian's. I thought you might be amused by it." She passed it across to him. "Look, there's me at the back. I can't remember where you were sitting; are you somewhere there too?"

He looked hard at the photo.

"I think I got cut out," he said. "I was over the other side of the classroom, if you remember."

He looked again, this time more closely. In the picture she looked as small and defensive as he remembered, dark-haired and skinny. He looked back at the person in front of him, comparing. Not the same girl now, he thought. Still had the same dark hair, although she was wearing it long today. The memory of her face, and especially her flashing angry eyes, gradually came into focus in his mind. Yes, he thought he could see traces there still. He wanted to say "What a huge improvement!" but thought better of it – it wouldn't have been so courteous after all. Instead he said:

"Your hair's much longer and thicker now, it's nice. And I've noticed you smile a lot more than you used to."

"Thank you. So kind," she said in mock gratitude. She added, with a frown: "They weren't the happiest days for me, you know." But then she gave him a warm smile in acknowledging the compliment.

He grinned back. "We used to think you were quite posh. With hindsight, you clearly weren't – just a solid middle-class girl who happened to have come from a school where they all spoke better." He laughed. "Trouble was, the difference stood out a mile, back then, and you know what kids are like for being able to gang up and pick on one person."

"And don't I know it! I certainly found out the hard way. Well, it had one particular effect on me," she said, suddenly hard. "It made me determined not to be beaten by anyone ever again."

Toby raised his eyebrows at that.

"Oh, I don't mean bullying or competitive sport or anything like that. I mean, why should people think they're better than me just because they had things and I didn't – at that particular time, you understand. I didn't want to be outdone by anyone, didn't want them to look down on me. So if people started to brag at me about what *they*'d got or where *they*'d been, I'd make up that I had something like that or had been there too."

"How long did that last?" he asked, suddenly quite interested. He was beginning to put two and two together.

She paused before answering. Then she took a deep breath, as if resolved, and looked at him straight in the eyes, almost defiantly. He thought he'd seen *that* look many years ago, back in school.

"I'm going to be honest with you. It became something of a compulsion."

But then she looked down at her hands, at once in some embarrassment.

"I'm afraid I find I still do it without thinking. Oh, I know I shouldn't, and I don't really need to these days. But it's become a bit of an automatic reaction, and once you've said something, it's really difficult to take it back. So you don't, and you decide to let them go on thinking you're clever, or well-off or well-travelled, or whatever. Even high-powered" she added sheepishly.

So *that*'s it! he thought. So she really isn't so sure of herself still. He looked back at her, feeling a moment of pity for her.

"I'm sorry. That's actually a bit tough, isn't it. Poor you."

He then had a flash-back.

"I remember thinking back then, that first time, how brave you must have been to stand up in front of the class and to be as honest as you were. If it's any consolation, I think you've just been equally brave to admit all that to me, especially when you didn't need to. You could have just said nothing."

She would not look at him. He supposed she must be feeling ashamed.

"Hey, Frances," he said gently. "It's alright, really it is. We're friends, aren't we? What you've just come out with, you've shared with a friend, OK?"

Now she looked back at him.

"Thank you" she said simply, with a quiet dignity.

"Look," he said, "I'm on your side now, alright?" She half-nodded but did not reply.

"You know, when we had that first long conversation on the coach, you had me wondering a few times. You were saying things about some of those places which weren't quite correct and I couldn't work out if it was just a slip of the tongue or a mistake or maybe you just didn't know. Not that it matters to me one bit, you understand, but now I'm thinking: did you ever actually go to the Taj Mahal or to Boston in the States? Or to the Serengeti? And I'm suspecting the answer's No. Or at least, not yet anyway. Am I right?"

"Yes" she mumbled, blushing.

"Don't get me wrong. I'm not judging" he was quick to add. And then, the big one.

"So maybe you aren't a Forex trader after all, because you didn't seem to know about arbitrage."

She nodded, looking down again.

"But how come you know so much about Amex cheques and dollar exchanges?"

"I wasn't being entirely untruthful, Toby," she said, with some spirit. "I do work for Lloyds, and I do handle most of the currency transactions." She paused, and then admitted: "It's just that I work in a Lloyds branch bank in the Southwark area, which is how I know all the admin procedures I was telling you about." A look of defiance came back to her eyes. "So, does that make a difference?" She was immediately hard, challenging him.

"Hey, whoa there! Don't shoot!" said Toby, holding his hands up in mock-surrender. "What can I say? You're still you. You've just been through a bit of soul-searching, that's all, and I respect that. I'm still looking at the same person who helped make my six days in France much more pleasant. And haven't I made a new friend? And I'd rather be sitting here talking to the real you than to a defensive wall based on inaccurate information."

"A defensive wall?"

"Oh, you know, always trying to guard against being challenged about something you might have said which wasn't altogether correct."

They were interrupted briefly by the waiter returning to clear away their starter.

Frances sat there silently.

"Look, Frances" said Toby. "I'm sorry if I've said the wrong thing – spoken out of turn. Have I messed up already?"

She didn't answer immediately but looked at him, considering.

"No, I don't think so," she said after a moment. "In fact, I feel almost relieved that I've told you. Yes, I know I didn't have to, and it hurt to admit it to you but, well, perhaps honesty really is the best policy after all."

"So," he returned, "speaking as a friend, let me ask you if you'll still carry on in the future in the same way. Or let me put it another way: as a friend, could I maybe encourage you to feel that you don't actually need to do it any more, in fact not at all. That you're OK as you are?"

"You might," she said. "It'd mean I'd have to learn to believe in myself all over again."

"There you go! No reason not to. You're obviously strong enough. You've still got that spark of defiance – I saw it again just a few minutes ago! I think you can do it. You've just got to want to." He stopped, realising. "Aagh, sorry, me being preachy. Apologies, don't mind me. What do I know?" The apology was genuine but he thought it would be safer to lighten the mood. He knuckled his forehead like a servant to his master showing that he 'knew his place'. "Sorry. Didn't mean nuffink by it, honest, your Ladyship!"

Which made her smile again.

At that moment, the waiter brought their main course.

"So," said Toby, beginning again. "Tell me about Frances. Why use your second name, and what was wrong with 'Rowena'?"

"Oh well, you know," she replied. "To me, 'Rowena' is not particularly weird, I admit, but it's pretty unusual, and definitely not in fashion. It wasn't exactly cool back then when we were young. So you risk getting laughed at just because of your name. And then you'd always get some kids who would call out Ro-*weeen*-a, and you can guess the nickname coming from that."

Toby thought he'd better not mention the unkind nickname they had for her at St Ninian's: 'Orphan', with a heavy stress on the first syllable.

She continued:

"So I swapped to my second name as soon as I moved schools – told them that my preferred name was Frances, and it seemed to work. Of course, I was far too young to know about Fanny Hill so had no idea what I was letting myself in for with 'Frances'. Which is why I was so tetchily particular when I introduced myself back in France. Not many people get to call me 'Fanny' twice!" she said grimly. "So then you get people like Claude calling me 'Fran' because it sounds different and maybe they think it's a more cool name. But I don't like it any more than the others. I know Claude means well, but she'd never take any notice in any case, so I let her get away with it." She looked at him. "How about you? Are you going to take a risk? Lots to choose from," she challenged.

"Who? Me?" said Toby. "Well, I already told you I prefer the name 'Frances' to the others. As for 'Rowena', I've always felt it has an unusual charm of its own, almost historical, though I can't think why. But I appreciate your take on it. It's *your* name, for goodness sake, so it's your wishes that matter. After all, people should be allowed to decide on their own name, if nothing else."

"Quite."

"So. What do we talk about next?"

Toby was anxious to move on from what was clearly a touchy subject with her. He thought quickly.

"So, now that you're back home and have had time to reflect, what did you think about Normandy as a taster for France?"

"How can I say about the rest of the country? I liked what I saw generally, but it can't all be like that. Or can it? No, of course not! For example, that whole area around Chartres was pretty boring, wasn't it? On the other hand, you see a lot of films and documentaries for regions like Provence, Burgundy, the Loire, the Dordogne, and they all look pretty fab. So, yes, I think I'd like to go further afield sometime and explore France some more."

"Sounds like a good idea, maybe for next summer? I guess you could always ask Claude to go with you – if you're still friends by then, of course."

She nodded, shrugging her shoulders non-committally. She thought for a moment.

"In fact, I went to the Channel Islands with her once – Jersey, it was," she remembered. "A few years ago now. Just a week. It worked out OK between us."

She paused, considering.

"The thing about Claude is: I never felt I had to pretend with her. The school connection counts for a lot still. I don't think she cared one way or the other about what I had done with my life since then or what deep and dark problems I might have. I mean, she just breezes along and doesn't show any interest in asking awkward questions.

She's very Easy-come Easy-go, is Claude. That's helped me."

"You know, I'm glad to hear that, after everything you've told me," said Toby. "It's good to know that you've had at least some support for what must have been a tricky problem over the years. It's a pity that a single year at St Ninian's caused all that trouble later. It shouldn't happen like that."

He was genuinely sympathetic.

"OK, so where else interesting have you been?" he said, brightly.

"What? Apart from the obligatory trip with everyone else to Newquay after A-levels?" she replied, sardonically. "Spain, of course. Who hasn't? But not Costa Brava or the Costa del Criminal. Barcelona was the obvious choice. And spending a few days in Madrid was worth it. Oh yes, and I went with my father on a short trip to Brussels, though I can't remember now why he was sent there - something bank-related, obviously. That's when I thought I might be able to go on to Bruges or Antwerp but it didn't happen. Shame," she added.

"Did you go to Spain with Claude?"

"No. My parents fixed up for me to stay with some people, to give me the chance to have a holiday with a bit of culture. Turned out to be lots of it in the end!" she laughed.

They finished their main course and decided to stay for coffee before winding the evening up.

Toby announced:

"You know, I went to Majorca on a family holiday after my A-levels, but I've never been to mainland Spain. As for Belgium, well, trips to Bruges seem to be ten-a-penny, and the pictures you see of it always make it look attractive and worth going to. Antwerp too, though I haven't been to either of those places yet. Often thought I might like to."

Then, on a sudden whim, he said:

"Just an idea, but if you ever think of going, what about, you know, we could go together? If you wanted to and were interested?"

What was he thinking of? He hardly knew her and he was suggesting something like this already? Just because he was enjoying her company again? On the other hand, why not?

"It could be fun," he went on, "and we could share costs like meals and such. We could try organising it ourselves, or else go on one of those trips which are relatively inexpensive these days, and single room supplements aren't that much more, so you wouldn't have to worry about, you know ….. No obligation, of course. You don't even have to consider it."

He grinned.

"And you can trust I'd be like Claude – no awkward questions, and you could just be yourself. No pressures, no pretences or anything like that."

"Well, it's an idea, and I can always think about it at least, whatever the outcome. As you say, there's no obligation. But thanks for the suggestion. And it's nice to know that someone else has confidence in me, I mean, isn't bothered by what you now know about me."

"Right!" said Toby. "Moving swiftly on ….. Did you want some more coffee? No? Then shall we get the bill? And do you want to go Dutch or split the bill?"

"I'd prefer going Dutch, if you don't mind."

"That's fine," he said. "I'll do the tip, then."

"No, it's OK. I'll put something in too."

"As you wish. Not something to fall out over, after we've had such a pleasant evening. Well,

I mean, I have. Was it alright for you too?" he added hopefully.

"Yes, Toby Stannard, thank you. I wasn't sure how it was going to work out but it's been nice. But I do need to be making tracks about now so the sooner we get that bill the better."

They finally managed to catch the waiter's attention and settled up quickly. They parted company at the nearest tube station.

"Maybe we can do this again?" he asked.

"Give me a ring sometime," she called over her shoulder as she hurried down the stairs and disappeared into the Underground.

Chapter Five

Following up

It didn't take Toby long to decide that perhaps, after all, he would quite like to see Frances again, and over the next couple of months he would phone to suggest that they meet up in their lunch hour, if only to chat and have a sandwich together. Being initially reticent, she found excuses to say No, but he persisted until she finally gave in. It was easy to meet outside Southwark cathedral to start with. Autumn was already advanced by then, and they could go in or stay outside, as the mood – and the weather - found them, and Frances soon became more natural with him and relaxed in his company. On one occasion they decided to meet up at the nearby Clink Prison Museum "just for a laugh". On another, they tried the equally close Old Operating Theatre Museum and Herb Garret on the other side of the cathedral.

Toby decided to take the plunge and ask Frances out for another meal. He didn't have a concrete reason this time, as he had on the previous occasion, but hoped that she was now happy enough in his company that he wouldn't be required to produce one. "OK. When and where?" she said, straight and direct, no messing.

"Oh, er, how about Friday evening, after work? And we could go back to the same Italian as last time or somewhere quite different if you prefer."

"How about going for a curry?" she offered. "It's December, and it's cold and gloomy. Plenty of places to choose from – I know several around here. You're happy to go Dutch again?"

"Fine, to both. You choose, and you can take me wherever. It'll be a surprise. Only, make sure it's reasonably close to a tube station – on your line? – for getting home afterwards."

Friday evening came, and they were in the Curry House ordering drinks and food. He chose a mild curry and a light-strength lager. Frances went for a much hotter dish and, slightly to his surprise, a large glass of house red. The curry portions turned out to be very generous and he wondered if she would get through all of hers, but said nothing. He just hoped she wasn't playing the "Trying Hard to Impress" game. She was wearing her hair tied back tightly into a single long pigtail, which made her look untypically severe.

The conversation inevitably turned back to the Normandy tour and their previous meal together.

"So tell me honestly," he opened, "what did you think of all those vast buildings. Do you actually like cathedrals?"

"Don't you?" she replied, turning the question back on him. He nodded. She continued: "Yes, well I suppose I do really, although it's things like the stained glass inside, and ornate clocks and such that I like best. You?"

"Oh," he said, "what I like to see are outwardly solid structures with ornate towers and spires, with strong columns supporting high naves inside. And wooden-panelled chancels with well-lit choir stalls. Very English, I know, but I was certainly interested to compare the grander French cathedrals."

"And have you changed your preference as a result of that trip?"

"No, not at all in the end, despite being highly impressed as I was with every place we saw in France. I think I really do need to go back and have another wider look at the country. Next proper holiday, maybe" he added, as an afterthought.

He was looking into the middle distance as he spoke, and the conversation faltered. He came to and looked across at Frances. She too was miles away at that moment, with a troubled look on her face. She was remembering something else, and he wasn't prepared for the complete change of subject when it came.

"I guess it wasn't very clever of me, trying to pretend and make out that I knew all about Bunker Hill and had been up it, when you had already told me you had actually been there."

"Yes. And, you know, it really isn't much of a hill. I mean, it's not high like you have to climb up it. It's more an area of rising ground which you walk 'on' rather than 'up'."

"So how did you come to be there in the first place?" she asked.

"Oh, it was part of my 21st Birthday present, made possible because of an American pen pal of my mother's who I think must have been persuaded by said mater to invite me over for a fortnight's holiday during that summer's vac. To "broaden my education" presumably! They were very kind and hospitable to me while I was there and I still keep in touch – occasionally. But I haven't been back."

"So what month's your birthday then?" she asked him, suddenly altogether direct again.

Taken aback for a moment by her forwardness, he answered:

"Well, actually I've got one coming up next month fairly early in the New Year."

"So that'll make you a Capricorn. I'm a Taurus myself. So would you say you were a typical Capricorn?"

"Yes, I guess so, if you believe all the stuff you read."

"So what's your Ascendant? Do you know?"

He looked blank.

"Why? Does it matter?"

"Only that it's the other main determinant of character and personality," she told him. "I could tell a lot more about you with that extra information."

"What? Don't tell me you work undercover for the CIA?"

"No. I'm just interested, that's all."

"Phew! Then I'll take that as a sort of compliment, if I may. Hang on to 'em when you get 'em, I say." She could see he was laughing at himself.

They ate in silence for a little while.

He found himself remembering those other 'inaccuracies' that she'd come out with on the coach that day. He spoke.

"Sorry for the reminder but, last time at the Italian, you admitted you hadn't been to India either. So I'm curious about what made you think of Jaipur when you were talking about the Taj Mahal?"

"Oh, that! I suppose I must have been thinking of the film, you know, the Marigold Hotel one which was supposed to be set in Jaipur. I love that film."

"Me too," agreed Toby, eagerly.

"But," he added, "here's a strange thing. If you look it up on IMDB, it'll tell you that the 'hotel' was located in Jaipur, as per the film. But if you do a search in Google for the location of the place, that entry says that it was actually in a village called Khempur, about 1½ hours drive from Udaipur, which is somewhere quite different, although all those places are in the same state, you know, Rajasthan. So which one do you believe?"

This being a rhetorical question, Frances could hardly answer it. So she just nodded. After all, it was just a film.

They ate, she with a certain amount of gusto. Her glass of wine was suddenly empty and she ordered a second. He looked at her closely. She seemed quite OK. Perhaps she was one of those slim girls who could pack away any amount of food – and drink as well – and it never showed? So, again, he let it go without a word. Instead he raised the subject of where she might live.

"So did you end up choosing a Curry House near a tube station on your line, like I suggested? I notice the closest station to here's on the Northern."

"What's this? The Spanish Inquisition? I didn't expect ……."

And then she laughed and said:

"Sorry, just a joke. I wasn't really annoyed. Yes, as it happens, I did, because I live close to Balham tube so it's really convenient. Oh, and I share a flat with two other girls, to save you asking!"

Said with a smile, so he assumed she didn't think he was fishing.

"Well, thanks," he replied. "You didn't know but that's done me a favour as I go down to Morden on the same line – I live between there and South Merton overground station. So it's good for me too."

"And you live amongst the baked beans with a flat-load of blokes? Or maybe in a cosy ménage à deux with your girlfriend?"

Now, was *that* fishing? All the same, he coloured a little at it – after all, he was nearly 29 and still without a long-term girlfriend.

"No, I'm lucky. I'm on my own in a small one-bed studio apartment – it doesn't really class as a flat. But there's a separate living area with a kitchenette. There's a shower. And a loo. So could be a whole lot worse. I'm happy with my own company." He meant, I'd rather not share a flat unless I absolutely had to – all those separate lives under the same roof, no thanks. But he kept that thought to himself and anyway he guessed it was different for girls so he didn't try explaining.

"But you're not a loner, are you? That's obvious from the Tour in September. You're really quite a sociable guy."

"I like to think so. What I should have said is that I feel equally happy on my own. But I would say that I prefer one-to-one friendships rather than that blokey thing of all going round in a gang together. Maybe you're the same, or similar at least, given your friendship with Claude. And doubtless you have plenty of other friends too."

"Yes. Well, maybe not "plenty" exactly. But enough, anyway." She seemed keen to change the subject.

"A propos of nothing in particular," he suddenly began, "I've been looking at how you've got your hair today. Ever tried that style where you plait the front in two and fasten the braids at the back? You see it sometimes - I've noticed it especially at some weddings. Personally, I quite like it. But," he added quickly, "not that you have to take any notice of me, of course."

He waited to see if she would react angrily at the suggestion and come back at him. He was relieved when she took it calmly enough and answered:

"Well, I don't normally wear it like this, but it was just one of those days when I got irritated with it and wanted some sort of change. And I was in a hurry this morning. I'll stay like this for the rest of the day, and then see how I feel again tomorrow. Funny," she went on, "I assume men do notice these things when they look at girls, but they don't usually comment. You're a bit unusual like that."

He raised his eyebrows at her use of the word "unusual" in describing him.

"No, like I said, you're a bit unusual, out of the ordinary maybe, so that makes you interesting in my book."

She gave him a direct look and smiled. Then changed tack abruptly again.

"Come on. Hurry up and finish! I reckon I had

twice as much on my plate as you did and I still finished first! Let's have another drink."

"Hold on, old thing. You've already downed two large glasses of wine."

"So who's driving? We'll be on the tube. Anyway, I don't want more wine, I want a Bailey's. What'll you have?" And she called the waiter over immediately and ordered one. Toby thought one of them at least should maintain a clear head so simply ordered a coffee. She sank her Bailey's in the time it took him to drink his coffee and before he could advise her against it, she had ordered a second one. Again, he asked for coffee.

"We'll make this absolutely the last one," he told her firmly and, in truth, the extent of her liberal consumption was beginning to show on her. She knocked back her drink quicker than she should, perhaps realising it was high time she was starting for home. They were able to settle the bill satisfactorily without mishap, and he helped her on with her coat. As she walked towards the exit, her steps were sometimes unsteady so he steered her out clasping her arm in his. Neither of them was prepared for the sharp shock of the winter cold outside hitting them after the heat of the restaurant. They had not gone many yards down the road towards the Undergound when Frances staggered and twisted sideways as they passed an alleyway.

And was violently sick.

Luckily into the alley and not all over Toby.

When it sounded - and looked - like she had thrown up just about the whole of the evening's menu, she managed to stand straight again, weakly, and as white as a sheet. And shivering.

Toby gave her his handkerchief – thankfully clean that evening – to wipe her mouth properly. He did not take it back!

"Right," he said. "That settles it. We take the same tube and I'm going to see you right to your door."

He took his coat off and draped it round her shoulders.

"Quick! get your arms into this. It's cold out here, and you're shivering hard."

She was in no state to refuse. He put his arm firmly round her shoulders and walked her to the Underground. At a kiosk before the ticket-barriers, he bought a bottle of water for her to drink straightaway and a packet of mints to help her feel a little fresher.

Fortunately there were not many stops between

there and Balham and, emerging from the station, she directed him across the Balham High Road and down past a couple of side roads before taking the third and then turning into one of the side streets off it. He was still bodily supporting her as they finally reached her house and she fumbled in her bag to find her latch key. He took it from her and opened the front door for her.

"Are you sure you can manage from here? Hopefully one of your mates will still be up?" said Toby anxiously. "I think you should make yourself a hot milky drink and fill a hot water bottle and go straight to bed."

She turned back to him.

"Thanks so much for all your help. I was enjoying myself too much, maybe. Do you want to come up?" she added weakly.

He declined the invitation as politely as he could.

She leaned forward as if she was about to kiss him goodbye and then, thankfully for him, thought better of it! Instead, she gave him a weak half-hug, followed by a wan smile, then went inside and closed the door.

He shrugged his shoulders, turned, and set off at a fast pace back to the Underground and homeward.

Chapter Six

Birthday Treats

Toby phoned the next day to see how Frances was after the curry episode. She had taken the day off as sick-leave but was already recovering. She assured him that she hadn't actually got food poisoning; she would have known, she said, and would have been suffering a lot worse if it had been. She reckoned she would be back at work on the following day, so he had no need to be concerned. Toby urged her to eat something nourishing but easy on the stomach – like scrambled eggs – just as soon as she felt able. She thanked him again for his help, but ended the call soon after, complaining of still being tired.

The Christmas rush was now on, and he didn't see her for the rest of the month. He phoned to wish her the usual 'Happy Christmas' but all he got was her voice-mail again. He did at least get a text reply from her which arrived just before the New Year, thanking him for his call and wishing him 'A Happy New Year' in return.

New Year's Day, spent with his family, had passed.

His 29th birthday was looming in the second week of the new month and it fell on a work day so he knew he wouldn't be celebrating with them until the following weekend. Not a milestone birthday, nothing whatever to make a fuss about, he thought, and so ruled out a pub celebration with his mates. He thought of Frances and another dinner-date but the memory of the previous month's disaster was still fresh in his mind and he definitely didn't want a repeat performance. Could she be trusted to be more sensible in future? He really didn't know her well enough to call it.

Still, he had to admit, until that point they had been getting on well enough. He was gradually learning more about her, and still finding her somewhat intriguing. It might be worth another go, if he politely laid down a few ground rules before they started, all to do with her alcohol consumption! Accordingly, he phoned with a tentative offer of another meal out, and he was surprised when she replied to her voice-mail almost by return.

"So what had you in mind?" she asked – which seemed to imply that she might well be up for it.

"Well, last time you chose," he said. "This time, it's my birthday so my terms – if the sound of that doesn't already put you off."

"Go on," she answered cautiously.

"OK, so you can still choose: from Italian, Indian, Chinese, English or French, but here's the deal. No more doubles or mixing your drinks. You know why, don't you?"

"Oh, swell! Don't remind me. Didn't I say Sorry enough the first time? Come on, be kind. Don't rub it in." There was a pause. "Alright, I admit it, I acted a bit shit in the end, didn't I?"

"No, you were never that". He tried to be encouraging, but he wanted her to be clear.

"Just don't do it again, OK? It's my birthday and I'd like to have a pleasant evening in the company of an interesting – no, an intriguing – person. That's you, by the way. So how about it? Easy terms or what?"

"I agree. Easy terms and I promise to be good, Sir. 'Swelp me, guv!" she added with a mock-cockney accent. "Would you prefer French or Chinese this time? It is your birthday, after all."

"Alright. Let's do Chinese. I'm partial to a bit of Sweet and Sour. OK with you?

"Sure," she replied. "And remind me, which day are we talking about?"

He told her, and added: "And no presents either. Just your company. And I'll pay for the pleasure – my treat; no going Dutch this time, alright?"

She consented.

"And I'll call for you around 7.30, if that'll give you enough time after work to get home and change. I know where you live, remember? I'll send you a quick text from Morden to let you know when I'm on the tube coming up to you."

"See you then," she said.

"See you then. Looking forward to it already." And he rang off.

So, on the evening in question, there he stood outside the house where he had left Frances on the previous occasion. He had timed his arrival for a couple of minutes after 7.30 – punctual enough, in his book. He thought she was not the sort of girl to demand his presence on the absolute dot. He realised he didn't know her flat number, but luckily one door-bell had 3 names against it, one of which was 'Brook', so he pressed it twice and waited for the intercom to engage.

"Hello? Is that you, Toby?" came the disembodied voice.

"Yes. Are you ready yet? I'll wait down here until you are. Don't be too long, it's pretty cold out here." He heard: "Coming right down," before the intercom clicked off. Minutes later, the front door burst open and Frances came bouncing out, all smiles and evidently pleased to see him again.

"Hi," she said, and immediately threw herself at him, arms around him to give him a big hug and a firm kiss on the cheek.

"Wow! Thanks" he said, steadying himself against the force of her show of affection. "What was that for?"

"Only what you deserve," she replied. "Just what I should have done last time, to say thank you. Only I was still so horrible and sicky, and couldn't risk passing anything on to you. I probably smelt pretty unpleasant too! You wouldn't have wanted a kiss from *that* now, would you? Would anyone?"

"I guess not" he answered. "Anyway, enough of that, it's history, OK? You're ready? Then let's get going."

She grabbed his arm playfully and hung on to him closely as they walked along to the Underground. Almost a snuggle. And not a bad way to start the evening, he thought. If she's happy, then it's going alright so far.

"Happy Birthday, by the way," she said. "So where are we going tonight?"

"I thought of that place in Southwark Street, which isn't far from the tube. Trip Advisor says it's a nice little 'no frills' restaurant with, quote, "very good food at a reasonable price".

"Sounds OK."

"Let's hope so." He paused, stopped briefly and looked at her. "Nice hair, by the way," he said admiringly. "I like it." And carried on walking.

"Thanks."

She took the compliment in her stride. "Hoped you would. Important to get it right, I thought." She was wearing her hair loose to the shoulder, held in place by a pair of braids from the front and pinned at the back.

"Did you need help with it or could you manage it all yourself?"

"Jane, one of my flatmates, she helped. She convinced me it wasn't such a crazy idea – you know, the one given to me by this nice weirdo I met up with last month."

"What? They're the *last* people you want to get involved with. Very dangerous, I'd say. Trusting weirdoes is always going to be a risky business. Did you come through the encounter unscathed?"

"Well, I did throw up *completely* at one point, which was pretty drastic, you have to admit. But strangely it didn't seem to put him off. And now, would you believe it, he's asked me out on a date to a Chinese, of all places!"

"Not the place we're heading for right now?" he said, in mock horror. "D'you think he'll be there tonight?"

"Oh, bound to be. Almost certain." Then, in a conspiratorial stage-whisper: "They say that he can't keep his hands off her!"

"Oh!" Toby reacted fast and let go of her straight away. "Sorry."

"Hey. No, I was only teasing. Come back, it's cold without your arm around me."

On the tube, she kept up the banter.

"Did you get any cards today? Or don't they bother to send birthday cards to Oldies like you?"

"What? Steady on, I'm only 29, thank you very much. So I'll have a lot less of the implied decrepitude, if you don't mind! In answer to your question, yes I did get five or six, from friends and various family members. That enough for you?" He paused. "So! Where's my card," he demanded theatrically.

"But I don't know your address, do I?" she retorted. "And, remember, you told me definitely no presents, so I didn't bring you one. You should have warned me."

"Quite right, quite right! Sorry. Anyway, who needs cards these days, especially with e-mail and the rest? And all that Christmas Card hype – ugh! Who needs all *that*?"

"A lot of people – me included – still like to get remembrances like that through the post. People who take that sort of extra effort tend to care more," she told him firmly.

"OK, White flag. I give in!" And then, in mock yokel: "Forgive me, yor ladyship, oi meant nothin' boi it."

"Well, Chivers," she assumed a haughty voice: "We'll say no more about it this time. But don't let me catch you with your hand in the biscuit barrel again! Otherwise Cook will have something to say about it!"

"No, Mistress, no!" came the servile reply, and they both giggled.

In due course they arrived at the restaurant. They were shown to a small table for two in a cosy corner with a single 90° bench seat, where the place settings were at right angles to each other instead of opposite. This forced them to sit close together, pretty well touching – there was no spare width for either of them to move away. They began by ordering drinks. As before, she had a house wine while he stuck to one of the asian beers on offer. After the waiter had taken their food order as well, he looked at her enquiringly. She knew exactly what this meant, and she assured him that she had learned her lesson so that Moderation would henceforth be the order of the day for her.

"Thank you," he said gently. "I believe you, and I do appreciate that. You never struck me as being anything but genuine, despite the other thing we've talked about, and I'm certain you're not one of those girls that does it to show off all the time. Were you maybe still nervous of me on that occasion, and somehow the control switch got sabotaged?"

"No, you're right, and I'm definitely *not* like that normally, and I'll prove it to you over time, if you'll let me. I think we're used to each other by now. I don't really know what came over me at the Curry House. Part of the old trouble rearing its ugly head again?"

"How so?"

Oh, you know, me trying to prove I'm just as good as the next man, that it's cool to drink big. 'Anything you can do ……..' and all that."

"But I wasn't competing. Wouldn't, in any case. And I don't see how I could have been encouraging you, either."

He paused.

"And anyway, I thought we'd got through all that stuff before then, remember? We'd talked about it and how you didn't need to do it any more."

He touched her hand lightly. He went on:

"I did tell you that I was already on your side. Maybe it was that you didn't really trust me and so were still a bit on edge inside, although you weren't showing it? I hope by now you can just be relaxed in my company. You know, natural. I'm quite happy with that kind of 'cool'."

She smiled gratefully at him and then raised her hand to brush his cheek briefly with her fingers. She picked up her wine glass, touched it to his own and, her eyes fixed on his, said softly "Happy

Birthday". She put her glass down again and, without warning, she half stood, leant across the table and kissed him full on the mouth. Almost as quickly, she sat down again, looking flushed, as if surprised by her own boldness. She lowered her eyes. "No presents," she murmured.

"No?" Toby said, momentarily stunned, but recovering fast. "Phew! That was ……. something else! Delicious, in fact."

He paused.

"Any chance of another? Any more where that came from?"

"Not at the moment, no" returned Frances who had recovered her composure equally quickly. "Here comes the waiter. Let's eat!"

In such a relatively confined space, he could feel the warmth of her through her skirt as his thigh was pressed against hers under the table. Was she feeling the same level of excitement as him? He had no way of knowing without asking, and he certainly wasn't going to do that and risk spoiling the evening before it had got properly under way. Luckily he could turn his attention to the food and drink in front of him. He found a new subject, a new question to ask her.

"Listen, it's my birthday so I'm going to ask, and hope you don't go ape afterwards but – and please think before answering – what would be your reaction if someone used your first name? I mean, if I – you know, maybe through a slip of the tongue? Would that really upset you?" He added hastily: "I'm not saying I would, but I'm curious to know how you might react if you heard it coming from someone like a particular friend."

She did not answer straightaway. He searched her face, suddenly worried that he might have gone too far and that she would have a go at him. He could not read her thoughts from her expression, but clearly she was thinking hard, which meant that he would get a frank answer.

"Honestly?" she said at last. "Well, seeing as it's you and I know you'd not be taking the mick, I suppose I could put up with it. But I think only in private, when it was just us two. I'm still Frances to the world at large and that's the way I want it to stay. Agreed?"

"OK, Chief," said Toby. "If I want another of those kisses from you sometime in the future, I'll do my best to stay in your good books. A price worth paying!"

"Who says you'll qualify for a second one? They're very rare, you know. Highly sort after and highly prized, dontcha know? They don't get given out lightly. And you'll have to join the queue."

"Aw, we're not on about that bloke again who you think is after you and who's supposed to be here at this restaurant tonight?"

"But of course," she countered. "Who else? I can tell you he's definitely in the queue for another kiss from me. You'd better be careful about him. They say he's very particular about the girls he queues up for."

"Yeah, well it's not his birthday, is it?"

"You don't know that. Might be. You can't be sure. Believe it or not, I *think* he might well have one around now. It'd be a remarkable coincidence!"

"Hmph!" Toby grunted, but secretly he was pleased with her banter. It was a good sign of how relaxed she was this evening with him. He switched tack again.

"There's something I've been thinking about mentioning, no, asking about really. Do you remember the conversation when you touched on a trip you once made to Brussels, and we talked about the popularity of trips to Bruges? I wondered what you thought about the possibility of us popping over together for one of those mini 3-night breaks if we could get a reasonably cheap deal. There are lots about, and I've seen one advertised on-line for travel and B&B at a 3-star hotel in the middle of the town for just over a couple of hundred each. I'd check about the availability of single-room occupancy beforehand, of course, and we'd be eating out, so there would be some extra cost for that. We'd travel by Eurostar all the way to Brussels, though our ticket would cover us for the whole return journey to Bruges, and a 3-night stay would give us a minimum of two full days there and also the latter part of Day 1."

"Or," he continued, "if that's more expensive than we can afford right now, here's a cheaper option. We drive there – I'll cover all the petrol but we go halves on the ferry - and book our own hotel. That way, the ferry would cost only £35 each and we could book two single rooms at the budget-priced Ibis for only about £120 each for the three nights. Plus the cost of eating out, which we'd obviously share. What do you think? I could bring my spare camera again, in case of a repeat accident. And my charger cable," he said enticingly.

Frances got the message immediately and

punched him playfully. "When were you thinking of doing this?"

"I thought maybe early March, say the Thursday to Sunday of the first full week. That way we'd need to take only two days out of our annual leave."

"Sounds almost tempting, but I'll need to mull it over," she said, after a few moments' thought.

"The thing is, the thing is …… do I like you enough? Do I trust you enough, more to the point?"

She leaned away from him, screwing up her eyes as if to assess him from a distance. She adopted the tone of an interviewer.

"Hmm. I understand you've come here today hoping to get a job as my escort to this particular town. Now I don't appear to have received your CV – not a good start, I must say."

She arched her fingertips and pursed her lips, giving him a fierce look of disapproval.

"So. I have a check-list here – it will have to do. First question: do you have all your own teeth?"

"Yes."

"Yes what?" she demanded acidly.

"Yes, m'm," he mumbled, in a suitably chastised way.

"What? Speak up, boy! Don't mumble like a half-wit!"

"Sorry, m'm," he muttered contritely.

"Good. If I'm to take on a thoroughbred, I insist on healthy mouthware. Now, young man, do you have your own i-Pod?"

"Yes, Matron. And my own charger."

She ticked her imaginary check-list.

"And gout – do you suffer from gout at all?"

"No, Matron," he mumbled again.

"An albatross. D'you have an albatross?"

"What?" he cried.

"An albatross, boy. Come on, what's the matter with you? It's a perfectly simple straightforward question. Do you own an albatross or not?" she demanded.

Again, Toby was secretly pleased with this display of a quirky sense of humour from her, and he was easily at home playing up to her game of nonsense.

"No, Miss. Not since I sprained me ankle one day at school, Miss. Since then, I ain't never touched a drop, Miss, nor ever had anyfink to do wiv' birds. An' I got a full set of me own marbles, an' all, Miss. Straight up I 'as!"

"Very good, Toby Stannard. Well, it says here that you've scored full marks so I think we can give you the job. Thousands disappointed, of course, but there can only be one winner, after all."

"That's alright, then," he said.

"Idiot!" she said affectionately.

"Idiot back!" he retorted, but equally warmly.

"So?" she said.

"So, does that mean you've decided that we might do this little trip together? Because I hope so, although maybe you should have more time than just a couple of minutes to think it over."

He put his hand over hers and gave it a slight squeeze.

"I really am house-trained, you know. If that doesn't sound too boring."

"Yes, Toby, I think we're OK with this one. Second option, though, please."

She gave him a winning smile. "Let's drink to it!"

Glasses were clinked, and they carried on eating for a while.

"So, who's this 'Matron'? Tell me about her."

"It's funny really," said Toby "now, looking back, we had a number of house matrons while I was away at boarding school but I can only remember the first one. I suppose maybe it was because she would certainly make the deepest impression if you're only 11 or 12."

"What was she like? Did I sound anything like her just then?" she asked.

"Good Lord, no!" laughed Toby. "Her name was Miss Pennyweather, I remember, and she was strong of arm and stern of manner. She was actually quite fair too, though you never saw that until afterwards when you'd moved on from her domain into one of the more senior boarding houses. She had a gimlet eye and could spot a guilty look in a boy a mile away! At least, we believed so. She ruled her boys with a rod of iron, although she was never nasty or vindictive. Many of the Old Boys still speak of her with genuine affection. And, yes, I was reminded of her when you said that bit about 'healthy mouths'. Strange how these things come back to you years later. Did you have someone in mind at that moment?"

"Oh yes, quite definitely! We had one teacher like that who behaved and spoke like she'd just come from riding with the Quorn – all frightfully hale, hearty and outdoors. Everything was very black-and-white with her, and if you didn't answer promptly enough she'd treat you like a simpleton. We used to call her the Sergeant-Major."

"Happy Days," he said, sardonically. She laughed, nodding in agreement.

The meal was almost over when Toby said: "So you didn't really mean "thousands" of admirers a little while ago?"

"Don't be silly!" she scoffed. "That would be completely absurd! What sort of girl do you think I am?"

She pretended indignation. "Not even hundreds. That was clearly a joke."

She paused.

"But don't go thinking you're the only boy to invite me out. I might be no glamour-puss, but I've had my fair share of men. Oh yes." This came out almost defiantly.

"It's OK. I believe you," grinned Toby, "though I'd rather not!"

"Meaning?" she demanded.

"Well, I'd prefer to think of you as having had experience of perhaps a few boyfriends rather than the picture of the number that "a fair share" conjures up! No man wants to see himself as just another in a long line of blokes, after all."

"Well, this isn't like that scene in 'Four Weddings and a Funeral' where he's sitting there in the café listening to how many men she's slept with," she retorted. "Give me *some* credit at least!"

"No, you know I didn't mean that," he said, trying to pacify her. "So when was your first, I mean, boyfriend?"

"My first? When I was 15, I had a crush on a boy who was only 16, but that didn't last beyond the following summer. Then I met another boy when I was in the Upper 6th Form and he lasted on and off through our college years, but he moved on without me at the end. Anyway, I picked myself up soon afterwards – not one to let the grass grow, me. Oh yes, there were others – including one proposal of marriage! But I turned him down."

"Really?" Toby tried to sound polite but was suspicious – that came out a bit too glib, he thought. He looked at her harder. "Really?" he repeated, more slowly this time.

"Yes, really!" She came back at him in a flash, her eyes flaring a spark of anger at the way he seemed to be doubting her word.

He softened his gaze. "*Really*?" he said gently. "Come on, I'm OK with it if it's true, but be honest with me. You turned him down. Why?"

"Because …. because I was unsure. Something about it, him, didn't feel as right as I thought it should. And he was a bit of a dominating personality, if you know what I mean." She sighed and sat staring down at her lap, her fingers starting to twist nervously. There was something in her sudden change of manner which made Toby suspect there was a lot of the story she wasn't telling him.

"Sounds like you did the right thing, then. Who was he?" Toby asked.

"Oh, a friend of my parents, in his late thirties. They thought he could help me with my problem psychologically, a bit like a therapist, although he's not professionally qualified. So I've seen him from time to time over the last couple of years, that is, I've had several sessions with him."

"You still see him?"

"Yes. Sort of," she mumbled. "I mean, on-and-off."

"Well, it must have done some good, because I think you've been doing pretty well, at least since last Autumn."

He tried to sound encouraging but couldn't help feeling that a slight shadow had fallen briefly over the proceedings.

Luckily, sitting so close as they were, it was easy for him to give her a sideways hug.

"Hey, it's OK. I'm no therapist either – not trying to be. But we've been here before, remember? Talked it through. So let it go. It's my birthday, and I'm just having a good time with you here. That's all that matters to me right now. Let's leave it at that."

He kissed the top of her head lightly.

"Come on. Let's order a coffee now, then we can get the bill and I can take you home."

She gave a little sniff, and then gave him a half-smile. She nodded her agreement. He gave her another reassuring squeeze and they ordered their coffee. He wanted to see her smile properly again.

"Thank you for sharing my birthday. I've had a great time this evening. Pity I can't have a birthday every month, but then, there's no guarantee you'd be free on all those other days – or even willing!"

"Hey, less of the melodrama, you!" she said. "Just be grateful I took pity on you and gave up a highly attractive alternative offer at The Palace this evening!"

"You had a better offer?"

"No, of course not. Only joking" she said gently. "Toby, thank you so much for a lovely meal. And I really am enjoying your company – and *so* much easier than The Palace!"

"Thanks for the compliment. And if I may be allowed to reciprocate, I think you are actually one of the most genuine girls I've met, and the Other Thing really is just so much water off the duck's back, as far as I'm concerned."

They finished their coffee and were soon on the tube back to Balham. Then down across the High Road and taking the third on the left. He waited while she found her front door key. "Do you have time to come in for another coffee or something?" she asked. "It'd be nice if the evening didn't have to end right now." She took his hand and drew him across the threshold before he had time to say no. "Come on up. We're on the second floor."

He followed her up the two flights of stairs and into her flat. Took his coat off and hung it up. He could see another girl in the kitchen.

"Hi Jane," called Frances. "You making coffee? This is Toby, by the way. Where's Kate?"

Jane only half-turned. "Hi Toby" she replied. "Kate? Oh she's out this evening."

"Is there enough water in the kettle for three mugs? Great. I'll come in and make an extra two for us. Shan't be a moment, Toby," and she went into the kitchen to help Jane.

Barely a minute later and she emerged with two mugs of coffee.

"Come on into my bedroom for a moment – I *have* got a small present for you after all, even though I know you said not."

He did as he was told and followed her in. She shut the door with her foot and put the mugs down on a small table. The room itself was not large, but big enough for a small armchair at the end of the single bed, and a tallboy next to a narrow wardrobe.

"Make yourself comfortable in the armchair while I find your present."

She turned away from him until he was settled in the chair, then turned back and climbed onto his lap, put her arms round his neck, and gave him a long kiss.

"Happy Birthday, Toby," she whispered in his ear, sending delightful waves down his chest.

Then, "I think you deserved that in return for a super evening. And thank you for coming up with the idea of a Bruges trip – I'd like to go there with you."

"Sorry," said Toby. "I missed most of that. Can we start from the bit where you kissed me?"

She repeated the pleasure.

Hardly had that kiss finished when Toby said "My turn," took her head in his hands and drew her mouth down to his, acutely aware of the softness of her lips. Instead of a drawn-out kiss, he kept the pressure of his own lips light on hers, lingering, and brushing gently from side to side, all the time encouraging her to kiss him back. He could not believe how eager she was. How many boyfriends had she *really* had? Not so many, he felt sure about that. But she was, quite simply, delicious in his arms.

They were forced to pause for air.

"No question, that is without doubt the absolutely best birthday present I've ever had," he told her.

"Good," she replied. "I made it myself. Only the best ingredients went into it. I'm so glad you like it."

She snuggled down against his chest. After a while he felt her wriggle in his lap, and then was aware that she was drawing down the zip of his flies. Her hand twisted around inside his trousers searching – and immediately came up against the hardness it was looking for. Toby had been full and erect since they started kissing but had managed to stay out of danger down below by concentrating on her lips up above. But now it was a different matter.

"I'm glad to see you're well equipped," she murmured happily. But Toby couldn't afford to take any chances.

"Thanks for the endorsement," he replied.

"But, look, Frances, I haven't come prepared, if you know what I mean, and there's absolutely no way I'm going to mess you about. Your hand feels fabulous down there, but I really do need you to stop before I lose all self-control. Put him away. Please."

She heard the urgency in his voice and reluctantly withdrew her hand. She did it slowly, to tease him a little longer, and was equally slow in zipping up his trousers again.

"Don't be a Delilah tonight," he pleaded. "You've been brilliant, but don't let's ruin it by going too far."

"How far's that?" she teased him further.

"Far enough that your mother wouldn't like it. Or your father, for that matter. You've already become something special for me, and I want it to stay that way. One step at a time, and all that. Please?"

She pouted momentarily, but then smiled and said: "I'll try not to be too disappointed. I'll just have to think of a plan to win you round."

"Oh, I think I'm 'won', all right," he replied. "I just don't want to move at rocket speed and risk messing up two people's lives for the sake of not putting the brakes on now and then."

He paused, wanting to change the subject, to break the prevailing mood without upsetting her. He said:

"Now, I'll bet my coffee's cold. Yours too."

And of course they were.

"Look," he said, " Don't bother about more coffee. Let me get off home now, and I'll set about getting some accurate quotes for the ferry and Bruges hotel for those dates in March. Can you let me know tomorrow if you can get those two days off work as annual leave? I'll obviously book nothing until we can both firm up on those dates. Or how about the following week, if there's going to be a problem with the first one?"

"Alright," she agreed. "I'll call you. I've got your number from the voice-mail on my mobile."

They emerged from her bedroom and he got his coat. He called 'Goodbye' to Jane who was still in the sitting room, and then had a last hug and kiss with Frances before setting out in the cold back to the Underground and Morden.

Chapter Seven

Bombshells

Toby waited for Frances to confirm which two days she could take as leave before approaching his own manager. Nothing happened for several days. Well, he told himself, wheels probably turn pretty slowly in a bank. But another week passed, and still no contact from Frances. In the following week he phoned twice but could only leave messages on her voice-mail. Finally, in the last week of the month, a voice-mail message came through from her to his mobile. But all it said was: "Toby, so sorry not to have replied. Problems here. Speak to you later." That was all; no explanation. Was there a problem for her at work or was she having unspecified problems herself? Or had she got cold feet after getting so much closer to him on his birthday?

January passed into February and still no proper contact. He made three calls to her mobile – all reaching only her voice-mail. He tried to sound conciliatory, caring. Was she in trouble? Did she need help? Could he do anything? But it was difficult when you had nothing to go on and could really only ask questions. He sent a Valentine's

Day card for the middle of the month, more than half-hoping she might have sent at least a text with similar sentiments to him. Still nothing. Then, the week after, out of the blue came another text from her. He read it, dumbfounded.

"Hi Toby, sorry am such a coward. Think im pregnant. So sorry. F."

"You THINK?" he texted back instantly. He couldn't take it in. She had to be joking, surely?

"AM pregnant i mean. God wot a mess. Sorry." came the immediate response.

"You mean me? We didnt get so far."

"No not you, someone else."

"???????" He pressed Send. He didn't know what to say in reply but couldn't end the conversation there.

"And got engaged, to therapist bloke. So so sorry. Bye."

"Bye? Wait! What? I mean congrats." Shit! He swore as he sent the text.

But once again his mobile fell silent. Not another text or call came from her.

What on earth was going on? One minute we seem to be getting on like a house on fire and the next minute she's engaged to some bloke *and* pregnant with it! I call and I text but she's clearly cut off all diplomatic relations – she's certainly shown no signs of wanting to see me or even talk to me. Thoughts like these went round and round in his head getting nowhere. Should he go round to her flat and try to see her, to get some sort of explanation face-to-face? Didn't she owe him that at least?

But what would be the point? If she's engaged now, she's looking to another man, and his turning up would only threaten to compromise her, and anyway would make him look pretty wet, a real loser, like a rejected suitor. Hell, it's not as if they had any firm relationship to hang his hat on – after all, they'd barely reached first base on that one single occasion. No, he'd just have to pull himself together and move on. Thank goodness he hadn't booked that Bruges trip in advance, he told himself.

He started to dial her number a few times but each time he chickened out and cancelled before the ring-tones. However, on one call, he completed the number, waited, and she answered. Except that it wasn't Frances; it was Jane's voice.

"I saw it was you so I picked up. Sorry, Toby, she's not here at the moment. She's just gone out to the supermarket – back in about an hour, maybe. Lucky for you she forgot her phone, which is unusual for her. So, can I help?"

"Oh hi, Jane. Thanks for picking up. Can you help? Now *there's* a question!" He couldn't help the note of heavy sarcasm.

"I know we weren't exactly an item, but what's going on? What's happened? How could she get engaged so suddenly? Surely not to that therapist guy, the one she'd turned down before? Why *him*?"

"Oh well," said Jane, "she knew him before. Seems he pressed his attentions around Christmas time, got her inebriated, then pregnant –"

"*Inebriated*? Don't you mean drunk?" he broke in.

"I suppose so."

"Was she sick all over him?" He couldn't resist it.

"What? Oh, you mean, like that time with you? She told me she didn't actually throw up over you."

"Well she certainly decorated the pavement!"

"Anyway, no, I don't think so. She discovered it just a few days after she'd seen you on your birthday. So then she told him about the pregnancy, and he said that perhaps it was time she reconsidered his previous proposal in the light of that. I'm paraphrasing, of course. Apparently she said yes, hence the engagement. It's quite a decent ring, too. Mind you, she's giving a good impression of not being exactly over the moon about it, not the happiest bunny in the warren! About either situation. Still, there you are …… Sorry, Toby, got to go. Nice talking to you. I'll tell her you rang but don't expect a reply. She's all at sixes and sevens right now and I think she's finding it hard to talk to anyone about it. Including me. So long. Bye."

He sat stunned. He felt strangely cheated and let down. True they *weren't* an established couple, but she had given him every possible indication, including all the kissing on his birthday, that they were moving towards it. But now he knew differently: that is, not two weeks before that particular day she had let this bloke get her into bed and she had had a whole lot more than a treatment - she'd had the full works.

Jeez! he swore angrily. And what sort of prat does that make me? He told himself he couldn't possibly have known unless she'd told him – which of course she wouldn't have done – but he still felt a complete fool, a prize idiot, as if he somehow *had* known and had acquiesced. Which was ridiculous. But he still felt as if he'd been kicked in the stomach.

What had she been thinking, all the time they were together that evening, having such a good time?

More to the point, what had she been thinking about *him*? Had she been privately laughing at him the whole time? Or just using him? Maybe she was trying to blot out the memory of what had happened to her just days previously. Or maybe – his brain was going into overdrive now - maybe she was aiming to get him to have sex with her in her flat that evening, and then be able to pretend later that it was him who was the father. Hang on, he told himself, but she didn't yet know she was pregnant at that point – she only found out days later. Still ….

And round and round his brain whirled until he gave up and went out, just to get a change of scenery and to quieten down. Perhaps he'd be able to think straighter tomorrow. What a complete mess. But, he quickly realised, that was far more the case for her than for him. He was just feeling rejected and sorry for himself, which he was forced to admit was nothing compared to the state of mind and body she must be in at the moment. Unless of course she actually *wants* to be married to this bloke, with a baby on her hands? But hadn't Jane said Frances wasn't happy about the whole business? Maybe she just meant the prospect of a baby and that Frances was happy enough about the bloke? No, Toby really didn't want to go down that road. Time to wake up, wise up, get a grip, and Move On.

And that was that.

For the time being, at least.

*   *   *   *   *

Four more months passed and Toby's life was getting back on an even keel. Spring moved into Summer, and with the much kinder weather he was feeling so much more positive. Even so, the memory of Frances grew larger in his mind as the time lengthened since his birthday, indeed as it does to all those who see themselves as having been dumped emotionally. He increased his efforts to counter this and force her to the back of his mind. And would have succeeded better if his mother, in his periodic phone calls to her, had not felt it necessary to badger him with unsubtle hints and questions about the state of his love life, if indeed he had one. Still, he accepted that Frances was not after all any part of his life and he turned to other interests.

As a result, he didn't go looking for fresh talent or try to revive a relationship with any past girlfriend. Let it lie a few more months, he said, and maybe start again in the Autumn. Meanwhile, I've a summer holiday to think about. And the more he thought, the more the idea of France kept returning to his mind, inevitably peppered with mental images of Frances in Normandy, despite his efforts to suppress thoughts of her.

He wanted a coastal holiday in sunshine and warm weather rather than blazing mid-summer heat. If it was to be France, he knew he would have to wait until the French family holidays finished at the end of August. So he booked a fortnight's annual leave from work at the start of September, and set about finding a suitable sea-based location, somewhere he could drive to with certainly no more than a single overnight stop en route. He pored over his map of France and quickly chose the west coast. But for warmth and better weather it would have to be south of the Loire, and also further south than the windy Vendée.

His eye fell on La Rochelle, which he remembered

from his studies of European History at school. Then he spotted an island just off the coast and right next to the city: the Ile de Ré. He searched on Google for more information and found it described as a French summer holiday paradise during July and August but otherwise remarkably under-populated by holiday makers outside of those months. The September climate there was reported to be good and there seemed to be an interesting variety of places, beaches and – what's this? – cycle paths everywhere.

The more he read about the island and its facilities and attractions for holiday makers, and that it was joined to the mainland by a bridge rather than a cross-water ferry service, the more he liked the idea of trying a fortnight there outside of the high season. He would drive down, of course, and could overnight in a B&B which could be fun and would add to the interest of the holiday. Far cheaper than a hotel and far more relaxing than trying to do the whole trip in one go.

Accordingly, he booked a small 1-bedroom studio apartment on the island, planning it just for himself, having decided he would welcome the time to be on his own: to relax, to bathe, to read, and play his own music. In other words, he would please himself for two weeks of R&R. And nearer the time, he'd find a handy B&B to book for maybe halfway down on the journey, and do the same for the way back.

He felt so much better for having got this holiday all sorted out and, at the same time, felt that he was winning the battle of getting Frances out of his system altogether. So it helped him not one bit when, one evening at the end of June, he got on his usual tube home after work, sat down and saw her, across the aisle and further down the carriage. She was deep in her book and didn't see him. Immediately his composure fell apart and his brain went into a spin. Hell! Should he remain undiscovered by her and let her walk out of his life again without even a word?

All the unanswered questions came crashing to the surface, but could he honestly accost her now after all this time and confront her with them? No, of course he couldn't; she was someone else's. But he'd seen her again and suddenly wanted desperately for her at least to acknowledge him. He stole surreptitious glances towards her but she was sitting too many seats away for him to see how far on she was, knowing as he did that she must now be something over six months pregnant.

He made up his mind. He would risk total embarrassment but he could at least ask courteously after her welfare, if nothing else. He saw her get up to leave the carriage at Balham and quickly followed her onto the platform, keeping a safe distance but ensuring she stayed in sight. She was not moving fast and seemed to climb the stairs wearily, holding onto the side rail. Wary of her pregnancy, he did not want to alarm or, worse, to shock her but he knew her route home well enough now and decided to follow, getting gradually closer, and to make contact once she was across the High Road.

It was the pedestrian crossing which gave him his chance. He caught up with her on the far side. He touched her arm and said gently: "Hi Frances. It's Toby. Can you stop a mo'?"

She froze for a moment, then turned slowly round to look at him, other pedestrians passing either side of them.

"Oh Toby!" She snatched her breath. "What on earth are you doing here?"

She looked hard at him.

"Have you been following me?" she demanded.

Instead of answering her question, he noticed something about her which made him stand and stare open-mouthed at her stomach and at her left hand. Suddenly pulling himself together, he drew her to the side of the pavement and blurted out: "You're not very big for 6 months! And where's your ring?" Immediately realising how unforgivably rude this must have sounded and what an oaf he must look like to her, he blushed furiously and stammered his apologies.

But no angry outburst of "How *dare* you!" or "Leave me alone" from her. Instead, tears welled in her eyes and through gritted teeth she threw her words angrily back at him.

"No ring! *No* baby! *Get it*?"

And then, more brokenly,

"Oh Toby, I'm so very sorry for what's happened."

"I don't understand" was all he could find to say, stupidly.

"Of *course* you don't! How could you? Toby, I can't talk right now. I don't want to talk to you now. Go back to the tube. Please just let me go home. And stay away from me. Please. I'm not worth it."

And, sobbing, she turned and hurried away down the road, leaving him standing aghast.

Suddenly, as if someone had snapped their fingers in front of his eyes, he came to and ran after her, catching her up as she turned into her road. Taking her arm he said:

"It's alright, I just want to see you safely home. I'll not say anything else, and then I'll leave you alone. I'm sorry, but I couldn't just ignore you after seeing you by chance on the tube tonight."

He escorted her up to her front door, waited while she found her keys, then turned without another word and walked away from her, feeling absolutely lousy.

He had gone about ten paces when he heard her shout his name and then the sound of running footsteps. She quickly caught up with him.

"Toby! Toby, please. I really need to talk to you, I've been wanting to for so long but I've been such a total coward. But I can't, not here, not now. When you get home, please phone me. I'll be waiting for your call and I promise this time I really will answer it."

And with that she squeezed his hand before running back to her house and disappearing indoors like a scared rabbit.

What *is* going on? he thought. Buggered if I know! And carried on walking.

Chapter Eight

Attempting Convalescence

On his way home, to say that Toby was suspicious of the situation, and of Frances herself, was putting it mildly. None of this made any sense without a lot of questions being answered. And even if she gave him answers, what then? Would he be able to believe what she told him? Would it be the truth? And even if he did get the truth, how would he feel about her then? Could he actually trust her again, especially knowing what she had done only days before she had really turned the charm on him?

He knew that he didn't have to contact her when he got home, or tomorrow, or ever. He had made her no promises, and she didn't know where he lived so couldn't come after him. His sense of injured male pride was sitting firmly on his left shoulder, whispering in his ear and tempting him to have nothing more to do with her. And yet.

And yet, the voice in his right ear reminded him that Jane had indicated how unhappy Frances had been. True, Frances had told him to stay away from her, but her agitated tone as she said this made him think that this was a typically female plea meaning just the opposite. And her last words to him sounded like a genuine cry for help which he would be a brute to ignore, despite the situation now.

He could not deny that he wanted, no, he needed the answers to his questions, whatever the outcome. And so he was not really surprised to find himself dialling her number soon after getting home. She answered straightaway, relief clearly in her voice.

"Oh Toby. Thank you so much for phoning. I had almost convinced myself that you wouldn't, and that you'd decide to have nothing more to do with me. Believe me, I'm truly grateful." She sounded it.

"I know you must be feeling really mad at me right now – you probably have for the last six horrible months, but I do so need you to let me give you some explanations. I owe you that much."

"Yes, I rather think you do," he said, wanting at that moment to be hard on her, even to find some way of hurting her, but not really being able to. He didn't know why but suddenly he felt a strong sense of pity for her, and the moment passed.

"Frances, I do need to know what's happened to you and how things got like this for you. And now that we're talking again, I'll not be able to stay away from you like you asked until I've got the full story. And I promise I *will* leave you alone properly if that's what you want. But right now I'm just confused about it all."

"Yes, it's a total mess, isn't it? But can we meet, if only for a drink together? We can talk about it, you can get your answers, and then I can be out of your hair after that."

You mean, *you* can be rid of *me*, he thought. But instead he said:

"I agree. A drink this time but no restaurant. You name a quiet bar somewhere near you and I'll meet you there. And we should agree on a date soon so that neither of us has time to get cold feet and decide not to show."

"OK. How about tomorrow evening after work? If we go to the pub round the corner from here, it should be pretty quiet, being a Tuesday night. We can go in the bar that doesn't have the football on the big screen."

She named the pub and gave him the address.

"Right, got that," said Toby. "I'll see you there tomorrow. Say at 7 o'clock?"

She agreed, thanked him again, and rang off.

The next evening, he strolled into the pub at the appointed time to find Frances already there, sitting at a discreet table in the corner of the Snug. He waved to her, saw that she had already got a drink, so got a pint for himself from the bar and came over to join her. They smiled at each other but he didn't kiss her in greeting and kept a certain distance between them as he sat down opposite her.

"You look different, tired, sad," he opened. "How these last five or six months must have changed you, put so much strain on you."

He did not say how much older she looked, which would have been unkind although true. Instead he tried to sound sympathetic.

"And I appreciate having the chance to see you again."

He paused.

"So this is where I would normally say "And it's been far too long," but given the recent circumstances I realise that might not be entirely appropriate. After all, I never thought to see you again after your news bombshell back in February."

"Yes, you're right about the strain, and inevitably I have changed, on the outside at least. But the peculiar way it's turned out, I'm just starting to feel I've a good chance of getting the real me back, I mean, back to how I was before it all happened. You need to let me tell you the whole story and I hope, by the end of it, you won't feel so inclined to condemn me."

"I'm all ears," said Toby. "But I warn you, there may be a lot of interruptions from The Floor."

"Well, try not to do it too often; otherwise I shall start to get annoyed with you, and I do need to get to the end so you have the full sorry saga before you go."

"OK, Rowena Frances. Off you go." And it had better be good, he thought.

She took a deep breath and began.

"So firstly, how did the calamity happen in the first place? And Toby, I warn you, you'll not be seeing me in a good light. I suppose I brought it all on myself, and all because of this insecurity and lack of self-confidence I've had all these years since school days. That's why I'd been having these sort-of counselling sessions from this older man my parents knew as a friend and who thought he would make a useful informal therapist for me. Over a fair number of sessions and visits to our house, when I had to go home each time for them, he took more than a shine to me. But he's a strong character and I had begun to see how he could get a bit controlling when he gets the chance. Which is why I turned him down when he proposed originally, like I told you."

"How old, exactly?"

"Oh, in his late thirties. But he was persistent. And could be very persuasive. He obviously jumped at the chance when my parents invited him to stay with us for New Year – they must have told him about how I sicked up all over the place after eating and drinking too much that time at the Curry House with you. Perhaps they thought I needed another 'treatment' from him."

"Anyway, the long and the short of it is, I'm so embarrassed to say, that one evening he got me drunk and we, you know, ended up in his bed going the whole way. Unprotected sex, you understand. He probably planned it all. I was pretty ashamed of myself afterwards and prayed that nothing would come of it. I honestly didn't know what the consequences would turn out to be when I was with you on your birthday."

"Were you being so nice to me because you wanted to blot out the memory of that night at New Year?"

"Yes. No. Well, yes I suppose I did, in part. But I liked you for yourself and because you never judged me or thought less of me because of my problem. I valued that, and wanted to show my appreciation by helping you have a nice birthday. That was the honest truth, believe me. And then you told me you thought I was a genuine sort of person, remember? I loved you just at that moment for saying and, I thought, meaning it."

"Well, I did mean it." He wanted to add: Except, I'm not so sure now, but he wisely kept quiet.

"And, yes, I would have gone to bed with you if you had asked me, because I liked you. A lot, by then. But I see now that would have been a big mistake for the two of us. So I'm glad, on reflection, that you clearly weren't ready and you stopped me from going too far with you. In the light of what I'd done only recently before that, and then what I found out a few days later, you would have felt terribly used, and that would have been so unjust."

"Well, I did wonder," he put in sarcastically, "you know, while I was upset about it and my brain was running wildly in overdrive. Sorry. Do go on."

Frances threw him a look of irritated impatience and then continued.

"So, back to the shadows. Only a few days after your birthday, I missed a period. Now I'm sure you know that isn't automatically a disaster, and so I was only quietly concerned but not actively worried at that point, if you understand me."

He nodded.

"Missing the second period – that's the dangerous one. And I did, the next month. I got your Valentine's card, by the way – it was sweet of you, but I was starting to get nervous and flustered by then so was distracted from reciprocating. I took a pregnancy test the next day which turned out positive. And, Toby, I panicked. Totally panicked. I knew who was the father, obviously, and contacted him straight away. I should have twigged there and then when he didn't sound in the least bit surprised and said: "Well, then perhaps you'd better agree to marry me after all! I'm ready and willing if you are." And – God forgive me – in my panic, all I could think to do was to say Yes to him."

"And there I was, suddenly engaged with a ring on my finger – part of his property now – and with a bun in the oven. And how could I possibly tell you? So I took the coward's way out and left you high and dry without a word from me. I'm so sorry."

"He actually regarded you as his property? Unbe-*liev*-able!" Toby cried out. Other people in the bar looked round briefly, startled at the sudden loud outburst coming from the table over in the corner.

Frances ignored the stares. She went on:

"So I finally plucked up courage to tell you the barest facts – I was too scared and distracted to tell you any more, and I couldn't face seeing you or talking to you. It was all too late anyway. For a while I was at my wits' end. But over the next few weeks I gradually got used to it. I didn't really get any proper Morning Sickness, just a slight queasiness to begin with, which I thought slightly odd. And then, over the next month or so, I had this weird feeling that nothing was actually happening inside me. But the test I'd done had definitely shown positive, so I must be pregnant, right?"

"Then one day in April, some time after Easter, I was talking about it to Jane and she said why didn't I do another pregnancy test? What would be the point? I asked. "Oh, I don't know," she said, "but it might tell you something." So I did, and I was amazed when it turned out negative!

I took an extra test the next day and that was negative too."

"So I went and saw my GP who confirmed that, if I had been before, I was now no longer pregnant. He explained that a pregnancy may be initially detected by an early test, giving a positive result. But if a later test gives a negative result, it's the later result which is more likely to be the true situation – so that I was indeed no longer pregnant. It didn't mean that the first positive test was wrong. It was just an early test which detected the first stages of pregnancy. He said that many pregnancies don't make it beyond the first few weeks, and I was one of those cases."

"Hence the lack of a bump now after all this time," said Toby. "But why didn't you tell me then?"

"Why should I? I was somebody else's woman now, and you weren't around any more. No, my problem was with You Know Who. I told him the news immediately and he made it clear he didn't care. In fact, he was very dismissive about the whole thing and showed no concern whatsoever for what my body had been through in those early months. Not to mention the emotional stress. He even had the nerve to say that he'd got what he wanted, i.e. me, so none of it really mattered."

"So when I finally plucked up the courage to ask him why we needed to be engaged at all, he laughed at me and started to make life difficult, getting my parents to bring pressure on me to accept the situation on his behalf. And to start talking about wedding plans. Already, when we'd only been engaged for two months! And when they didn't stop, it really began to get to me."

"Poor old you," Toby said gently. "A real bummer of a situation!"

"Well, the end of this sad and sordid little story is that, only a fortnight ago, I made a big decision. I screwed up my courage and finally went to see him and confront him face-to-face. I told him I no longer considered myself engaged to him, did not want to be, and had no intention of marrying him now. I threw his ring back at him and ran like crazy. I've refused to answer the phone either to him or to my parents since, and it's been absolutely horrid. Jane's been a real brick over all this, right when I needed someone to lean on. I've even told Claude about it because I was so desperate to talk it over with a friend who wasn't involved in any of it."

"And then you turned up out of nowhere yesterday, and turned me all upside down inside – no wonder I was so upset. That was the very *last* thing I thought I needed. But now, talking to you like this and pouring out all my woes, I'm starting to wonder if maybe you can help me in some way, though I don't yet know how. Maybe you've been 'sent', like one of those angels. Have you been 'sent', Toby?"

And she gave him one of those hard questioning stares.

"Oh, well," he replied, cautiously, "that depends on what help you need and whether I can honestly give it. I think we need to talk a bit more, but not about all that. Get to know each other again a bit, don't you think?"

He was pleased to see her half-smile and nod at him.

"But first, let me get some more drinks. What'll you have? Same again?" She nodded and silently handed him her glass.

In a short while he was back from the bar with fresh drinks.

"Cheers," he said. "Let's see if we can get a bit more comfortable in each other's company and talk about ordinary things. Show me your hand a moment."

He took it in his and pretended to study it carefully, like a doctor.

"Good, good. No signs of nappy rash or incessant drudgery at the kitchen sink, I see. And that awful red rawness around your wrist made by your ex-fiancé's slave ring seems to be healing nicely. Do carry on using the cream I gave you, won't you." He thought it was a good time for flippancy.

She smiled at him.

"Idiot!" she said, starting to relax a little.

"Idiot back," he returned, with a grin.

There was a pause.

"So, how have you – damn, no! Sorry, that couldn't have been more gauche of me."

He tried again.

"It's good to see you again after all this time. Weird that it's only been six months and yet it feels like a lifetime. Well, not really, but you know what I mean. So much has occurred since January, even though most of it has been on your side of the tracks."

"Yes, well, these things happen," she said in a resigned tone of voice.

"Not to everybody," he said, sounding harder than he meant. "I'm just so sorry it had to happen to you."

"Thanks," she replied. "And I'm sorry about Bruges. Sorry that it didn't work out. It was a lovely idea."

"Yeah. Missed the boat on that one. It looked good on paper, at least," he added, ruefully. "Too bad. Some things can't be helped. You can't bring 'em back."

"Can't you?"

Toby chose to ignore this. He wasn't sure what he felt right now, but if she was hinting at further possibilities for them both, he remained wary of the idea of a renewed involvement with her. This current level of reconciliation was one thing, acceptable as it was, but don't let her think he was an emotional pushover. He didn't feel like getting any closer and was glad to have the small table between them. The actual gap was insignificant but at that moment it represented a safety barrier to him. Easier to walk away from her if he needed to.

The conversation seemed to stall. The silence began to feel awkward. He drank; she sipped. This time she took the plunge.

"So, here we are, it's almost July, and the holiday season's just about on us. Are you planning to go away anywhere?"

"Yes. And no prizes for guessing where. How about you?"

"I told you Claude's been helping me lately trying to get back on an even keel. You just might remember my mentioning the idea of exploring the Dordogne way back last year on the coach? Anyway, Claude came up with the same suggestion recently, so we're thinking about going down there for a week's touring together. It'll be good to get away from all this for a while. I'll take the usual holiday fortnight but haven't thought about the second week yet. The thing is, we'll be together for a week so we thought we'd hire a car and drive down, you know, so we could take time to see more of the countryside on the way before actually getting there."

"That sounds like a jolly good idea, I mean, for you to get away with a friend even if for only a week. But, if I may give you a piece of advice, I would strongly suggest delaying your trip until after July and August. Remember that these are the holiday months in France where everybody piles down to the holiday destinations – mostly coastal, I know, but the Dordogne is equally popular with the French as well as the English, as I expect you know. *I'm* taking my two weeks in France on the coast, though not nearly as far down as the Dordogne. I've booked for the beginning of September to be sure of avoiding the holiday crush."

"Oh, that sounds like good advice. Thank you. I'll pass it on to Claude right away. Are you going back to Normandy again?"

"No, further south, below the Loire. Well, the bottom of the Vendée, in fact. Near La Rochelle."

"Are you going tenting? Or taking a camper van?" she asked. "How will you get there?"

"I'll cross by the ferry or Tunnel and drive down – it'll be fun. I'm told, out of holiday time, the French roads are usually so much freer to drive on. I'll probably do an overnight stop at a B&B on the way down, just to add to the adventure. I'm renting a small 1-bedroom studio – ideal for one person, although it's advertised as having beds for three people!"

"You're not going with someone else, a friend, a mate?"

"No. I want a quiet time and, remember, I'm very happy with my own company. And it'll give me time to think, to take stock. And to do a lot of reading for pleasure, not to mention sea-bathing. And there's cycling, of course. I found out you can hire bikes very easily and the place is tailor-made for leisurely cycling around. The beaches look generally good. Yes, I reckon it'll be OK. Mind you, from what I can gather, there's stacks of interesting places to visit for the two of you down in the Dordogne. Chances are you'll have a great time. And probably just what you need at the moment. How do you think you'll travel?"

"Well, nothing's decided yet but we were thinking we might drive all the way. Or we could try to get a cheap flight for most of the way, hopefully as far as Bergerac; then we could hire a car from there for touring round the Dordogne itself. Like you, we'll investigate staying in one or more B&Bs while we're there – clearly it's the cheapest option."

"Sounds like a good plan," agreed Toby. "Well, good luck with that one!"

The conversation began to falter. Funny how suddenly you can't find a thing to say, he thought. Why can't I even make any smalltalk?

"So how's work?" he tried. Lame, but at least it was something.

"Oh, you know, same old, same old, although naturally being summer there's a lot more call for foreign currency, which is keeping me busier than usual at the moment."

"Of course," came back Toby but without any enthusiasm. He found himself remembering their early chats on the coach in Normandy and how she had bent the truth about her job in banking.

Frances looked across at him and saw that he was gazing into space. What was he thinking? she asked herself. What does he think of me? Oh Lord, he's miles away – probably lost interest by now. I wish he'd say something else – anything. Does he expect me to do all the talking? Suddenly he's not making it easy for me. Is it maybe time for me to cut and run? She considered her next move.

"Earth calling Toby, Earth calling Toby. Come in please!"

Toby jerked back to the present, to see her looking seriously at him.

"Look, Toby, do you want to go on with this? Or have you had enough?" Of me, she thought. "I'm grateful that we've done this – met again and talked, I mean. I told you. I needed to set the record straight with you about what happened, and I think I've done that. Whatever you think of me – and I really don't know what that is right now – I've been absolutely honest with you. No fabricating, no bullshit. It's been warts and all. We were on the way to becoming more than just friends, I think, and yes I recognise that the mistakes were mine, so maybe that means everything's changed now. I need – I mean, I'd like – some sort of clue from you so I know how you see it, how it is from your side. Do you want to make a clean break and say goodbye now and walk away? Or might we be able to stay friends at least?"

She left the question hanging in the air.

Toby looked back at her, saying nothing while he tried to collect his thoughts into some half-coherent answer. Finally, he took a big breath and replied:

"Well, since we're being honest, I'll admit that, before I saw you yesterday, I felt I had just about got you successfully out of my system after six months. It took quite a bit longer than I expected but I was, you know, getting there. But now ......" He sighed.

"Hang on," flared Frances. "We're not talking love affairs, broken promises, broken hearts here! Yes, I admit that this whole messy business knocked my self-confidence for six for a while, but I'm not looking to you to play Sir Galahad. I've been building myself back up without your help, may I remind you! And you're not the only pebble on the beach! We're just talking Friends, OK?"

She glared at him, challenging. Her eyes flashed momentary anger at him. And then her expression changed to one of pain.

"And another thing, while we're on the subject! You won't have the slightest idea about the emotional turmoil a thing like that caused me. How could you? Being a man, you won't have any conception of what it's like not wanting the new life which you believe is growing inside you. And yet you *have* to come to terms with it; you can't just deny it. It's unjust but you feel yourself focussing more and more on that new life alone."

"And I started to get used to the idea, to accept it, despite everything. I thought it was going to be real. Forget the man I didn't love, he was nothing to me. But a baby? So imagine the emotional jarring when you discover that it's all a mistake and the baby's not real after all, especially after the effort you've made to adjust to the idea of motherhood. Toby, that readjustment was hard! I felt the pain of loss as much as relief at my escape. Yes, for a while I did suffer inside, believe me!"

Humbled by her outburst, he apologised, although without knowing precisely what for, and asked for permission to continue. She gave it grumpily.

"Thank you for explaining all that to me; you're right, I had no idea," he said gently. "Although, in my defence, look at it from my point of view –"

"Toby Stannard!" she interrupted sharply, "this is *not* all about you!"

"No, I know, I know." He paused. "But you *did* ask."

"Yes, I did," she conceded. "You're right. Sorry."

He continued:

"There I was going along quite nicely, thank you, and certainly not going out of my way to find a new girlfriend. Then I meet this girl, quite by chance – turns out I knew her in a previous life. Over a few early encounters, I find out that she's nice. No Helen of Troy for sure, but nice-looking, a pretty decent figure, and a pleasing smile. What I would call, you know, nice. Anyway, I soon find out that she's got a few quirks: for example, she doesn't always observe her kerb drill in foreign towns, she has a good line in the occasional bit of exuberant pavement artistry when she's had more than she should, she's even been known to misrepresent the facts about certain famous places abroad. But underneath she comes across as a pretty genuine sort of person – and you don't always meet so many of those in your everyday life. So, like I say, I mean, she's nice."

"But then it turns out later that she's got a skeleton in her closet. A mistake in her past has caught up with her, seemingly with a vengeance. It's a private matter and nothing to do with him, as far as she's concerned. And she's right, of course. Then maybe she's afraid of what he'll think of her if she tells him? Best let him go his own way, she decides, and she should get on with tackling the change in her circumstances."

"And perhaps that would be fine, were it not for the fact that these two people had become friends without trying, and it seemed were already starting to move to the next stage. She had certainly upped her niceness towards him. OK, so what *is* he to think?"

He paused briefly.

"And what is he to think when he learns the facts and the significance of that mistake? No, don't answer that, because neither of them has the answer. Not yet, at any rate."

"So the upshot of this is that he finds that he hasn't got her out of his system after all. And, that he actually cares about what happened to her. He feels bad for her sake, although it's nothing to do with him. He also sees that it's not a question of blame – far from it - and, significantly, that none of the things he already knew about her beforehand have changed. Just her circumstances."

"And here's the thing: he's coming to realise that he still values her enough to want her friendship. It's just that those awkward circumstances have muddied the waters and he can't see what's best for her."

Or for him, he thought.

Now at last he was able to pose the important question to her.

"I appreciate your being honest with me. That's important to me. You ended by suggesting that we might be able to stay friends. But are the waters too muddy now? Have things moved on too far for you? Because if they have, I can thank you and simply walk away now. Clean solution, no uncertainties. I told you before, remember? that I wouldn't mess you about, and I'm not going to start now. The alternative, seeing if we can stay friends and doing things together from time to time might work too, but maybe there are already too many uncertainties in that option for us to handle?"

He sat back and waited for her response.

She stared at him hard, almost with a look of scorn.

"Toby Stannard," she exploded, "will you just *stop* being some sort of prize moronic prat?"

She sounded like she was mad at him now; or, he thought, was she just putting it on?

"What *is* the matter with you men? I really believe you wouldn't see an olive branch if it slapped you in the face! Look, I've admitted I made a massive mistake, and I told you that I'm getting over it. On my own. Without help from a man. I've asked if we could stay friends and you rabbit on about "muddied waters". I'm not rolling over and begging, if that's what you want! It's your life and *your* decision. Do you want to see me again regularly or not? If you're serious about Not Messing Me About, then for goodness' sake do buck up, get a shift on and decide one way or the other – I really haven't got all day!"

What? he thought. I try and give her some slack, and suddenly she makes out that *I'm* the idiot?

She was glaring at him, and then she softened and gave him an encouraging smile.

"Come on," she cajoled, after the pause. "Didn't you say you still liked me?"

"Yes," he croaked – his mouth was so dry by now.

"Sure." He drained his glass. And then more definitely: "Yes, I did, didn't I!"

"Well, then. Hurry up and buy me another drink! All this jawing and soul-searching is thirsty work. I'll have the same again, please! Chop, chop!" She thrust her glass out to him.

When he returned from the bar and sat down, they looked at each other and smiled, the relief apparent to both of them.

"Phew! Thank heavens we've got that over with," he grinned.

"Yeah, it's good to talk," she said with affectionate cynicism. "Men! Honestly! Anyway, Cheers!"

"Cheers!" he replied, and they clinked glasses. He asked her:

"Can I come round and sit next to you now? Less confrontational. More friendly."

She patted the bench seat beside her and smiled invitingly. He moved and sat next to her, but not as close as they once had been, months earlier. She did not shift her position to cosy up to him but instead let herself lean against him companionably.

"Getting any better?" he asked her.

"Yes, starting to feel better already," she answered. "You too?"

He nodded.

"I have to admit," she said, "that it's a huge weight off my mind. I'd got really worried about not telling you, not even contacting you."

"No, well, thanks" he replied. "I mean, the truth of what happened has been a bit of a shock – a lot to take in all at once. But, even knowing all that now, it feels a whole lot easier, I mean, about you."

He paused, thinking: And you've been bloody lucky, my girl. But instead, he said:

"If you ask me, I think it's a miracle the way things have turned out for you, and I'm relieved for you. And glad too. I'd be sorry to think of you raising a family you hadn't planned for – worse still if you had been forced into it against your will. Oh, damn, sorry, was that me going too far again?"

"No, it's alright. I know what you mean. But now it's time to close that chapter and start a fresh one."

At the same time she was thinking to herself: I reckon I was *so* incredibly fortunate to get off that lightly. Under normal circumstances I'd have been *really* caught and it would have been disastrous.

They were silent for a while. Then,

"And you'll let me walk you home?" he asked again. Although, not for anything more, he thought – he still wasn't entirely sure about her.

"Thank you, kind Sir!" she said, and then punched him playfully. "Don't be silly, of course I will. In any case, it's the very least a gentleman should do. I like it when you're a gentleman," she added.

"Have I ever been anything else?"

"No," she replied, suddenly serious, "I can't say you have." Then she gave him a grin. "So that's alright then."

It looked like the friendship was back on, for a while at any rate.

Chapter Nine

Toby's Idea

On the way back, arm-in-arm as friends, they talked some more about her unbelievable escape.

"Basically, I don't understand it," said Toby. "I mean, what do I know about all that sort of thing anyway, but it's not normal, is it? Certainly not usual."

"Right. But it happened. Obviously I could hardly believe it either, but I went on-line to check what I'd been told by the doctor. Lots of references on that precise subject came up, and it was just like he said. I guess I was just one of the few lucky ones."

"And thank goodness!" Toby answered.

They reached her front door, and she invited him up.

"Er, no thanks, all the same," he said apologetically.

"Oh?" she questioned.

"Well, er, it's not that I wouldn't like – I mean, you've given me quite a lot to think about, and I'd like to go away and do it while the information's still fresh. If I came up – well, we both know how enjoyably distracting you can be!" He grinned.

She smiled back at the compliment. "Oh alright then, I'll let you off. But let's meet up again soon, OK? Give me a bell."

He gave her a quick hug and turned to go.

"If I don't ring you first!" she called after him as he walked away on the now-familiar route back to the Underground.

*   *   *   *   *

In fact, it was only about ten days later when Toby found a good reason to contact her. "Phone asap. Have money-saving wheeze." he texted. Later that day she rang. He said:

"It's about your Dordogne holiday with Claude. I've had an idea which could save you quite a bit of money getting there, if you haven't already booked your travel."

"No we haven't right now, but we're meeting at the weekend to finalise the details of the journey. With only eight weeks to go, we need to get on and book things."

"OK, well, can you meet me straight after work? I need to be back home by 7.30 – going out at 8.00. So no time to lose! And bring a pen and paper with you so that you can write stuff down."

She agreed, and they arranged a convenient pub.

Later that day in said hostelry, drink in hand, she waited expectantly for him to begin.

He took a deep breath.

"My idea is this – and remember it's just an idea, a suggestion, and you don't have to go with it if you don't want to. Absolutely no obligation. Now, I started with your idea of possibly taking a budget flight - have you chosen where to yet?"

"No we haven't. Maybe Bergerac. Go on, get to the point!" she urged.

"So. You know how it's really cheap one-way but they sting you if you book a return flight?" He saw her nod in agreement. "So, I thought I'd go on-line and see what airports you could fly to. Brive looks nearest to the eastern end of the Dordogne region, Bergerac to the western end. But – and here's the point - you had said you wanted to see a bit more of the countryside en route. So then I thought: La Rochelle airport isn't that far away, so what if you hired a car from there instead?

I saw on-line that you can get car-hire from there like at most airports."

"And you said you were staying near La Rochelle at around the same time?"

"Right. So here's where you start noting things down. It suddenly occurred to me that I could save both of you the cost of the outward leg of the flight if you hitched a ride with me, from here. I'll have the cost of the whole drive to cover anyway regardless, including the Tunnel, so you could both travel as far as La Rochelle for free. I'll be driving right past the airport so I could drop you there. If you've booked your car on-line in advance, you can simply collect it then and continue on down to the Dordogne from there. At the end, you can return the car and take a one-way flight home, certainly at far less than the cost of a return flight. I know at least two budget airlines that fly to La Rochelle, although it depends where you'd want to fly back to in England, of course."

She wrote that down.

"How long would that take? Certainly an awful lot longer than a straight flight."

"Yes, I admit it would mean doing an overnight stop on the way, but you can get a double room in a motel or local-type accommodation for under

£50, which would be less than £25 each to share. I've checked out the route and I could get you to La Rochelle by late afternoon. You'd arrive only about an hour later than if you flew, but it does mean that you wouldn't reach the Dordogne in one single go. So, for that last part of the journey, again you could do a night's stop-over at a cheap motel or B&B, halving the cost each."

"Sure. So, we would have to leave home the day before?"

"Yes, I'm assuming we're both planning a Saturday-to-Saturday holiday there, so I'd pick you both up from here immediately after work on the Friday evening and we'd drive straight to Folkestone and the Tunnel. I reckon we'd be able to reach the motorway on the south side of Rouen before we needed to stop for the night. If we had an early breakfast and set off again by 9.00, we'd be at La Rochelle airport by 5.30. With your car pre-booked, you'd pick it up and be halfway to the Dordogne before you needed to stop again."

More writing. She was looking thoughtful about the idea.

He felt encouraged enough to add:

"I realise, of course, that the downside is having to spend so much time in my car with me driving, but you could alternate between the two of you over who sits in the front and who can have a switch-off period in the back, and when. But the upside is that you get to see a lot of France properly at ground level, right from the start, which you wouldn't do in a plane. Which you said you wanted to do," he reminded her.

"And you wouldn't charge us for a share of the petrol or the Tunnel crossing?"

"Like I said, I'd have to spend all that anyway, with or without you. But if it would help your holiday funds to go further by coming with me instead of taking a plane, then please consider my suggestion seriously when you talk to Claude."

"Well, I'll certainly talk it over with her. And she does sort of know you already, so you wouldn't be strangers. But I absolutely can't promise anything right now. I mean," she added, "I can't say definitely yet if we'll take you up on your idea."

"Of course not. All I ask is that you discuss it as soon as you can and, if you both decide to take up the offer, let me know quickly so that I can go ahead and find the cheapest overnight stop for us and book two rooms instead of one. I've already booked the Tunnel crossing; I'd just need to amend it to three people in the car, not one only.

The rest – booking a hire-car and a single flight home – will be up to you."

"OK, I'll do that this weekend when I see her. I think I've got all that, but if I've missed anything, I'll give you a bell or text you."

"Good. Can you think of anything else to ask me while we're here?"

"What about luggage? Would you have room in your car? How big is it?"

"Well, it's only a modest-sized hatchback. But if you flew, you'd each be restricted to a medium-size case and a cabin bag. I can't imagine you'd be wanting to take masses of clothes – it should be English summer temperatures down there in early September. So I'd put all my stuff behind the back seat, plus your cabin bags, and your two cases would sit beside whoever's in the back. I'm sure that would work OK."

"You seem to have thought of everything," she said, slightly accusingly.

"Once the idea came to me, I tried to think of all the angles you'd need to know. But, look, that's all it is; it doesn't come with any strings, and if you both decide No, then that's fine, and no-one's any the worse off."

"Fair enough. Like I said, it's not definite yet, but I'll let you know what we decide, hopefully by Sunday evening or Monday."

"Good. I'll look forward to your call. Now I need to drink up and go as soon as we're done here. Nice to see you again so soon, by the way."

"Thank you, and likewise. Yes, I'm just about finished too. Just give me a moment and I'll come with you as far as the Tube."

And together they left the pub, and parted company when she got off at her Balham stop.

*   *   *   *   *

Frances was as good as her word and got back to him late that Sunday evening. She phoned.

"Toby, hi, it's Frances. Well, Claude and I have had a long chat about your offer. I must say I was in two minds. I like the idea of getting there quickly, but the prospect of travelling more cheaply than we thought is appealing, and I did say that I'd like to see more of France on the way."

"OK," said Toby doubtfully, waiting to hear the "But, ……."

"Yes. But Claude was all for the idea; said she didn't mind the extra travelling time for doing it much more cheaply – and I think she maybe quite likes you!" she added, provocatively. "Personally, I don't know what it's going to be like cooped up with you in such a confined space for so many hours, but in the end I didn't want to disappoint her, so I agreed. In principle. Pending our own research for prices of single and return flights and where we could fly from. I have to admit that my holiday budget is none too generous – I think it's easier for Claude but she's voted for the cheaper option. So give us a couple of days more to do a bit of research for ourselves, and I'll aim to get an answer back to you on Wednesday, one way or the other. Agreed?"

"Agreed," said Toby, and they hung up.

On Wednesday evening, a text arrived from her: "OK you're on. Will come with you."

He texted back: "Great. Will let you know when motel booked + cost." Which he was able to do by that weekend.

Chapter Ten

Preparation and Unexpected Attention

A few days later, it occurred to Toby that perhaps the three of them might need to get together at some point to discuss details of the journey. Plenty of time yet, he thought, so he was surprised to get a text from Frances after only ten days or so. It read: "Phone me. Claude wants you." He was just as surprised at the mention of Claudia. Why? He phoned back the next day.

"What's all this about Claude? What does she want with me? Are you pulling my leg?"

"Like I said," came the reply. "Claude says she wants you." She said this teasingly. "By which, she means she wants to see you again. And it sounds like soon!" He could almost hear her laughing at him down the phone.

"Why? Whatever for? I haven't seen her for almost a year."

"Well, we talked about the trip, and she sounded awfully keen! She seems pretty enthusiastic about the whole thing! Come on, what's wrong with her? You're not frightened of her, are you?" Frances was clearly enjoying herself.

"No, of course not! But I don't see – Look, as a matter of fact," he went on, "I've been thinking that we need to have a get-together soon, maybe in your pub, to discuss the plan in detail. I can show you both the route I'm intending to take, and where I've booked the overnight stop. And it will give Claude a chance to quiz me on anything that's on her mind right now about the journey."

"OK, good idea. I'll see when she can make it – say, one evening after work again at the pub – my pub?"

"Fine. Let me know when. First half of next week would be alright for me."

"Right, got that. I'll get back to you soon," Frances said.

All of which left him wondering about Claudia and whether she had any weird designs on him, even though they'd only chatted properly the once, in Normandy nearly a year ago. This made him feel vaguely uneasy about meeting her again. Or was Frances just having a joke at his expense?

In due course they all met up after work at Frances' local on the agreed evening. He got there first. The two girls came in together; he was at the bar ordering a pint when they came up behind him. In total surprise, he was practically knocked off balance by Claudia who immediately threw herself at him, flinging her arms round him and giving him a mighty – and wet – kiss on the cheek. Momentarily pinioned by her, he looked helplessly at Frances who stood back, watching with evident amusement. She gave him a smile in greeting and then raised her eyes to the heavens melodramatically, pressing her hand to her heart as if to corroborate Claudia's show of passion.

"Hello Toby again! Long time no see!," gushed Claudia who luckily hadn't seen Frances' mocking gesture. "Super to meet up with you again at last! How *are* you?"

"Oh, er, hi Claude. Good to see you again too," Toby managed, disengaging himself from her embrace. He turned round to raise his eyebrows questioningly at Frances as if to say: what was all *that* about?

Frances it seemed was determined to milk this for a little longer. Winking at him, she suggested;

"Why don't I get some drinks and leave you two to cosy up? You must have *so* much to catch up on!"

She made a show of turning her back on them and calling over her shoulder: "Go and find a nice quiet corner to sit at – and don't wake the neighbours!" Claudia immediately responded by hugging Toby's arm and positively dragging him over to a corner table, making him sit beside her. His ale slopped alarmingly but he managed to save most of it from the enthusiasm of her greeting which he thought, frankly, was well over-the-top.

Luckily for Toby, such moments of ambiguous passion were curtailed by the arrival of Frances with drinks for her and Claudia. Once again she gave him an encouraging smile as she sat down.

"OK" she said matter-of-factly. "Now we're all together, Toby's going to talk about the trip in a bit more detail. But before he does, has anyone any new questions to ask?"

Claudia could hardly wait to get in first.

"It's really great of you to offer to let us come with you all that way and save on the air fare *and* see more of France into the bargain, Toby. Thanks *so* much!" Again the gush. "My first question is: what size case can I bring with me?"

Toby described the size of the area of the back seat behind the driver, where he intended to stow their two cases.

"Keeping the size down to the space available is more important than the weight of your case," he explained. "Your two cases need to be roughly the same size to fit into the space because we may have to stack one on top of the other. And of course it will be important to keep enough space clear on the other side so that whoever's travelling in the back will be as comfortable as possible. I'm intending to put in a light rug and a couple of small cushions for the back seat, in case you want to close your eyes and get your head down on the way. The first leg of the journey over in France is all motorway, for two hours, to Rouen, so it should be a smooth ride if either of you wants to rest."

"And what about rest stops, you know, for comfort breaks?" she went on. "Will they be few and far-between?"

"From what I can gather, the service areas, the *Aires*, seem to be relatively frequent, at least on the motorways. Once we get off the motorways, we'll have to look out for public toilets in the towns, I guess."

"So where have you booked us to stay overnight? Is breakfast included in the price?"

At this point, Frances broke in quietly:

"And Toby, please tell us how much we owe you for the overnight stop if you had to pay in advance. Or is it one where we pay on checking out?"

"Thanks, Frances." He smiled at her as much in gratitude for interrupting Claudia's monopolising of the floor as for appreciating her calm and undemonstrative presence.

"So, Claude, to answer your question, here's a map of our route and I've booked a couple of rooms in a Fasthotel about half-an-hour south of Rouen."

He unfolded a route map of France and pointed out the location.

"It's only 2-star so it'll be fairly basic. But it's just for one night. And with the cost of a room about £40, it should be only £20 or so each. The rooms are doubles, and they do have twin beds, but I hope you won't mind sharing a double bed if you find you don't get two singles. There's free wi-fi, and there's a restaurant for some food in the evening when we get there, and obviously for breakfast too. Meals not included at that price, of course, but breakfast is likely to be less than €10 for a standard continental breakfast. And we pay when we check out."

Frances asked again:

"Roughly what time do you expect we'll get there? I'm thinking of supper and whether the restaurant will still be open."

"Well, that depends on what time we get away from here to start with," answered Toby. "We'll need to get to Folkestone by 5.15 at the latest on the Friday afternoon, which means leaving here as close to 3.45 as we can. It's much earlier than we'd like, I know, but French time is an hour ahead and we'll need food when we arrive. So my plan is to drive up on the previous evening to load the car up – this means it'd be really helpful, Claude, if you could arrange to stay at Frances' place that evening so I could pack all your stuff in the car then. This would help a prompt getaway the next day. All being well on the French motorways, I'd expect to reach the Fasthotel around 10.15."

"That's pushing it a bit, Toby, isn't it?" Frances pointed out, with a worried look.

"Yes. Sorry about that – can't really be helped. By being half-an-hour south of Rouen when we start the next morning, we should be able to reach La Rochelle airport by the end of the afternoon, for you to pick up your hire car. Is there any chance of both of you getting permission to get off from work earlier than normal on the Friday? We really do need to start by late afternoon if we're to have a chance of a meal when we arrive."

"Well, I'm not sure right now if we can. What do you think?" Frances turned to Claudia. "But surely it's worth a try at least. I for one wouldn't be able to take an extra half-day's leave on that Friday, but there's always a chance that I might be able to wangle an hour if I do someone else's lunchtime shift. How about you, Claude?"

"Sure, I don't mind trying," she said enthusiastically.

"OK," continued Frances, "let's make some tentative enquiries about it. I'm pretty sure at this stage we'd get no firm promise from our managers, so most likely we won't know until that final week. I'd certainly prefer it if we could get to our overnight stop earlier than 10.30 at night – surely not even a hotel restaurant would stay open that late?"

"Maybe not," agreed Toby, "so see what you can do nearer the time. We'll just have to leave that one open for the time being."

"Another question," put in Claudia. "Do we draw lots to see which of us gets to travel in the front with you? I'm looking forward to it already!"

Toby was getting alarmed by her seemingly mounting warmth towards him.

"Well, that's really up to you two. My own idea is that you would take it in turns; I mean, you could swap every hour or so, or do it to coincide with stops for comfort breaks. Or if one of you particularly feels the need for a bit of shut-eye in the back." He thought this might be more than likely if Claudia was part of the ride!

"And what about music on the journey?" This from Claudia again. "I presume your car plays cds?"

"Sure. And in case either of you hasn't got music on your phone, there's an iPod socket too. But I've no idea what sort of music either of you likes; and who's to say you'd like the sort of stuff I listen to? I don't want there to be any rows about what music gets played, unless everyone can agree. And I'm sure we wouldn't want it on all the time either. So it might be best if you bring your own music on your own device, and play it privately through ear-phones. Does that sound reasonable?"

The girls agreed.

"Anyone want another drink?" he asked them. He took their orders and escaped to the bar for a five-minute breather. Returning to the table, he found himself back in the spotlight immediately, as if Claudia couldn't wait. She demanded he sit close beside her again. Frances looked on, still with that amused look on her face.

"So. The route," Claudia started again. "Any nice places we'll be passing through en route? Show me on the map, Toby."

She snuggled closer to him, tucking her arm in his as if claiming him for herself. Toby glanced over at Frances with a look of panic, and mouthed the word 'Help!' at her. Her only response was to grin back at him, giving him a look in return which clearly said: Don't be such a baby! Claude won't bite! Then she briefly stuck her thumb in her mouth and sucked on it to show what she meant.

A fat lot of help *you* are, he thought. Better make the best of it, I suppose. He tried to concentrate on answering the question.

"Well, Claude, the idea of course is to try and get you two down to La Rochelle and your hire-car as quickly as possible, so I'm not expecting there to be any significant time for sight-seeing en route – although we will of course need to stop for lunch somewhere. But, to answer your question specifically, there are a few towns we'll be going through which might have something of interest in passing. Give me a bit of elbow room, Claude," and he managed to shrug her off sufficiently to reach into a pocket and pull out a piece of paper.

"I've made a summary of the planned route for you to take away. I've marked a few places: you'll see, for example, Pont de l'Arche where we cross the Seine, and later Mortagne and Bellême which look like nice towns. We'll be crossing the Loire at Saumur, which looks impressive. Then further down there's Thouars and Parthenay. Not that I've ever been there before, but it's great having Google Earth to have a look at them. You can do that too, between now and the trip, if you want to see for yourself."

He passed the list across to the girls.

"You'll see I've also marked some average travelling times between places, courtesy of Michelin's on-line Route Finder web page. And I've also jotted down a few of the things we've already talked about, like information on the name and place of the overnight stop, including a phone number and ETA based on the time of the Tunnel booking. Useful things like that."

"Thank you, Toby, that was thoughtful of you," said Frances. "Claude and I can look at it in more detail later."

"Yes, thanks so much for going to *all* this trouble just for us!" said Claudia warmly. "I knew you'd turn out to be an OK sort of guy. I can see this trip's going to be a great start to our week!" and she gave him an admiring look before planting another kiss on his cheek and hugging his arm.

"Right," said Toby, "well, I've been doing all the talking. Let me sit here and enjoy my drink while you both tell me about what you plan to get up to, I mean where you plan to go, in the Dordogne."

Once again, Claudia jumped in first so she could keep his attention focussed on her.

"It'll be our first time too, of course, but friends have strongly recommended various places to us to be sure to visit: Sarlat and Rocamadour, obviously; then there's La Roque-Gageac, Domme, Gourdon and Monpazier. I admit they're not much more than names at the moment, but we've seen pictures of the most famous places, which makes a good focal point for a first visit. That's right, isn't it, Fran?"

Toby saw Frances wince ever so slightly on hearing the name, but she just smiled and nodded. Evidently she was prepared to accept it from Claudia, though not from anyone else.

"Listen," he said. "I'm going to finish up here and

slip off home. Leave you two here until you're ready to leave. If there's anything at all about the plan or the details we've talked about that you want to query, don't hesitate to contact me."

Claudia immediately expressed disappointed at the prospect of his leaving so soon and looked as if she was going to pout.

"But it'll be easy to arrange another get-together like this if we need to. It's important for me to know that you're both absolutely happy about the trip."

At this, Claudia perked up.

"Oh I'm sure we'll need to do that. Won't we, Fran?" and she gave Frances a hard meaningful stare.

"Er, oh, yes!" agreed Frances hastily. They both stood up to say goodbye to Toby who, to tell the truth, felt as if he couldn't get away fast enough. A smile and a quick peck on the cheek from Frances, and a look which said: I'll give you a ring soon. In contrast, Claudia couldn't resist the showy hug and the wet kiss full on the mouth. Toby didn't respond but thanked them both and made a run for it as politely as he could!

*   *   *   *   *

Toby was back on the phone to Frances the next day.

"What was all *that* about?" he asked her indignantly. "You saw her. She was all over me. Like a nappy rash! Where did all that 'hanging on my every word' come from? I mean, she's nice enough, she's even not bad-looking, but, well, *really*! I mean to say!"

"Oh don't be such a wuss, Toby," came the reply. "Claude's alright really – you know she is. It's just her way with men she likes or latches on to. Some men like girls who gush over them."

"Well I didn't – don't!" he answered. "I don't think I'm shy, and I'm not usually with women. But she came on much too strong at me and I found it all a bit embarrassing, especially in front of you."

"You mean you were worried what *I* might think? Oh come on! She's my friend. So are you, for that matter. So she likes you. So what? *I* like you, although I'm not going on holiday with you. You never know – after a 2-day road trip with her, you might get to feel differently about her."

"Don't joke!" he came back quickly at her. "So

alright, it could turn out like that, I suppose. You have to accept that anything's possible, however unlikely. But if I was to be going on holiday with a girl – which I'm not, I might add, then I can tell you that Claude would not be at the top of my list. You know the sort of girl I'm drawn to, and she doesn't come close."

He realised what he'd just said.

"Don't tell her I said that, by the way! Promise?"

"Alright, I promise, though I'm sure she'd be devastated to know that's how you feel."

"Hey you, will you stop teasing yet?" Toby wanted this sort of talk to go away.

"Who's teasing?"

Still, Frances couldn't resist one more tweak on the nerve of his discomfort.

"She's always on the look-out for a good man, and I happen to think she'll be a good catch for most men."

Not for me, he thought, but instead retorted:

"Well I hope she finds him elsewhere and not here. Being friends with her might be OK, but nothing more. And that's flat!"

"Yes, sir. Anything you say, sir." She giggled at him down the phone. "Can I go now, Sir?"

"Yes, I guess so." Toby sighed. "No, wait! Sorry, I haven't asked how you are, how you're getting on. And are *you* any happier about the trip?"

"Stop worrying, I'm fine about the trip. Really. And stop worrying about *me*, I'm fine there too, although thank you for thinking of me."

"That's OK. I just like to know that you're alright – I've found I feel happier knowing there's nothing hurting you now." Or no-one, he thought. "So, anyway, thanks for listening – I think I've got Claude in perspective now. Maybe I'll even stop being a wuss!"

"That's the ticket! You've got it. Stand in front of the mirror every morning and say that to yourself between now and the trip. It's bound to do some good somewhere along the line!"

He knew she was still laughing at him but he did feel better for talking to her about it so he let it pass. They hung up.

Chapter Eleven

The Drive

Towards the end of the following month, the three of them met for a second session in the pub, mainly to check that everything was proceeding according to plan. Claudia was as over-attentive to him as before, but less gushy. Toby for his part decided to play along with it and so flirted mildly with her without, he hoped, giving her cause to think there was anything serious in it. Frances continued to take something of a back seat when Claudia was there too, and smiled quietly at Toby a lot of the time. She had at least stopped teasing him about Claudia which made him feel that maybe she was on his side after all.

*   *   *   *   *

And then, suddenly, the day of the trip was upon them. As promised, Toby had driven up to Balham on the previous evening to get the car loaded with their bags. And, as it happened, both girls had been able to leave work earlier on the Friday afternoon, having pleaded the importance of catching the precise channel crossing at the start of their holiday. Consequently, Toby had been able to pick them up from the Balham flat an hour ahead of the planned schedule. Friday afternoon traffic getting to the M20 was as busy as expected but thankfully it all kept moving and there were no incidents to delay their progress. As a result, they reached Folkestone and the Tunnel terminal sufficiently ahead of time to find that they had been given a crossing on the next train before their booked slot. They gained only a half-hour over their original schedule, but even this much was helpful for their onward journey.

Claudia had rushed to bag the front seat first, and had been animated and chatty for most of the drive to the Tunnel. She demanded to see his phone to find out what music he liked but he shook his head and instead pointed to the glove compartment where she found his iPod. After a while, when she'd run out of conversation temporarily, she spent ages searching through it. Occasionally she gave exclamations of agreement as she found an artist or group she liked, but mostly she called out names to Frances in the back from time to time to see if she agreed, or reacted at all. Toby glanced in his rear-view mirror to see Frances' reaction but she seemed to be deep in her own phone or simply staring out of the window, grunting to show that she'd heard Claudia's remarks.

When listening to Claudia's seemingly incessant supply of bright chatter and, like Frances, making the right noises to show he was listening, Toby thanked his lucky stars that cars no longer came with bench seats in the front. He felt so much more protected, even isolated, from her by having the gear stick and brake handle between them. He was good at concentrating on the driving and quickly learnt the art of switching to automatic listening pilot when she was talking. And in the early stages, once across the Channel, he could justifiably give the best part of his attention to now having to drive on the right.

As Toby had warned the girls, most of that evening's journey on the French side was on the motorway. And, for most of the way, there was not much excitement for the girls to look at, but there were enough service *Aires* en route for a comfort break whenever one was called for. After a week's work and the final rush to be away, the girls soon found themselves content to stare out of the window and watch the world rush by, or to relax and shut their eyes – after all, an hour on the M20 followed by two hours on French motorways, was not going to keep them riveted for long!

They didn't emerge from the Tunnel until 7.30, by which time the French traffic had eased considerably, so that their run down to Rouen was steady and uneventful. The girls had changed over in the Tunnel ready for the second leg. Once installed in the back, Claudia's chatter soon dried up, and Toby could relax. Given the difference between the two girls, he wanted to enjoy this session with Frances next to him. She was so much quieter and more thoughtful, which in itself was a pleasure as much as a relief! And it was nice the way the way she smiled at him when they occasionally caught each other's eye.

They were passing Boulogne and saw the start of the Péage ahead in the near distance. Suddenly, as they approached, they found themselves driving over the long and spectacular Echinghen viaduct. High above the valley as they were, they all fairly gaped at the view to the sea across to their right. Almost immediately, they had crossed to the far side and reached the toll barriers. With the car being a right-hand drive, Frances had to lean out to grab the motorway ticket. And, when they reached the southern end of the Péage section near Abbeville, Toby was on the wrong side for the toll, but she handled the payment on her side of the car without any fuss. They talked a little every so often, but the silences were equally companionable, and Toby was beginning to appreciate what a useful – he quickly corrected himself – no, an agreeable travelling companion she must be. Certainly a preferable alternative to Claudia!

They reached Rouen in just over the expected two hours and, with Frances' help, he negotiated a confusing junction at the bottom of the motorway to cross over onto the riverside road southwards to Port Saint-Ouen. Then it was a simple run down to cross the Seine at Pont de l'Arche and on to the hotel which they found easily just before the junction to cross the A13 motorway.

They arrived at the Fasthotel shortly after 10.15 and were relieved to be told there was a choice between a Buffalo Grill behind the hotel or a McDonalds just up the road where they could still get a late snack. As tired as they were, they decided on McDonalds in the hope of something light and quick. They dumped their overnight bags and trudged up the road, welcoming the chance to stretch their legs at least, after such a long time cooped up in the car.

Nobody spoke much for the next half hour or so while they ate and drank, and by common consent they were soon back at the hotel and getting off to bed immediately. They agreed to meet for breakfast at 7.30, for a 9.00 start, needing an early getaway the next morning. Their two rooms proved to be basically appointed but clean and good enough for what was required – a good night's sleep.

*   *   *   *   *

The following morning they set off with Claudia once again claiming the front seat first, so Toby was glad to be able to keep her mind occupied on negotiating the immediate junction ahead of them, to get across the A13 motorway successfully. He had seen on the Michelin web-site how tricky the junction looked. "Just concentrate on following any sign pointing to the N154 and Evreux," he told her. They got beyond the A13 without any trouble and only went round the next roundabout twice, looking for the right exit up onto the N154. They enjoyed the forested scenery away to the left as the broad dual carriageway wound its way southwards.

However, by the time they were passing Evreux on their right, it was drizzling hard and they almost missed the left-hand fork on the main junction where the right fork would have taken them westwards and way off their route. Just in time Claudia yelled a warning and Toby swerved the car left to regain the proper lane for continuing south. With relief, everyone relaxed and in another 15 minutes they had reached the N13 and were heading for Mortagne.

The countryside soon became much more interesting, the road stopped being a continuous and boring dual carriageway, and they felt as if they had at last reached proper rural France. The girls became much more chatty, and Toby was content just to drive on and listen to their excited remarks on the world now on view from the car. They reached Verneuil and he checked the petrol gauge. He knew that petrol was cheaper at hypermarkets and that he only had another 25 miles to drive before he got to Mortagne where – thanks again to the wonders of the Michelin route-finder web-site – he had seen a SuperU hypermarket on the way into the town, which also had petrol.

After filling up the car at Mortagne, he made the girls swap places, and was soon grateful to have Frances navigating beside him now. He found he needed help straightaway in getting through the town successfully to come out on the right road to

Bellême. It had looked straightforward enough on the map, but he had driven round the main town square twice and stopped at least once to check the map before she spotted an important road sign around the corner and hidden from view on their way into the square! "And not for the first time!" commented Toby in some exasperation.

After that, it was plain sailing out of the town, straight down to Bellême which was declared a pretty little town by the girls, and on southwards. Their route took them round the south side of Le Mans, and then down one of those typically long straight French roads; on the way they stopped for some lunch in the town of La Flèche which was attractively decked out everywhere with the municipality's colourful floral planting. After another hour, they finally reached the wide Loire and the crossing at Saumur. The tide was out as they drove over, and many sandbanks were exposed on the shallow river bed. The castle high up on the slopes behind the town looked inviting, and they all regretted that there was no time to stop and pay a visit.

Once again, the girls changed over at Saumur, and they were now on their way to Thouars. But it was Frances in the back who, after another 15 minutes, cried out as they passed by the town of

Montreuil-Bellay on their left. She had spotted a dramatic, almost fairy-tale, castle dominating the view. Her disappointment at having to leave it behind was evident, and Claudia tried to console her by saying that they ought to come back another year and explore that area.

After Thouars, it took another 40 minutes or so before they reached Parthenay. Claudia cleverly spotted a public toilet right on the roundabout coming into the town, which suddenly was exactly what they *all* decided they wanted just at that precise moment! To Toby's surprise, Claudia climbed into the back of the car straight afterwards, saying that she thought she had a headache coming on, and wanted to shut her eyes for a while. Frances fished around in her bag and offered a couple of pills which Claudia took gratefully before pulling her cap down over her eyes and settling back.

"How much longer do you think we have to go before we reach La Rochelle airport?" Frances asked Toby quietly.

"Oh, about 90 minutes, I reckon. Not much more. So not that long to go now, given how far we've come."

"That sounds good," she said. "I think you've driven us very well, so I'm not criticising in the least. But it has really been quite a long time in the car with the two of you, and I'll be ready for a fresh change for the last leg of our trip to the Dordogne. No offence."

"None taken. I didn't know how this trip was going to work out, but I think we've done pretty well. Threesomes can be quite tricky, can't they? But no arguments, no major fallings-out, no-one at anyone else's throat! I call that a success."

"Yes, I do too. So thank you," and she gave him a quick kiss on the cheek.

"Why, thank *you*," he replied and saw her looking at him with genuine affection in her eyes. For a moment he felt himself melting inside and then quickly pulled himself together.

"Time to be off again."

They got back in the car and set off with Frances now beside him in the front, and Claudia quiet in the back. Toby felt lighter, better. And once again Frances proved her value as a navigator when they arrived at Niort and had to find their way round the west side of the town heading for the N11. No road number signs any more; they found themselves searching for signs pointing to La Rochelle – easy enough, if only you could spot them! Just when they thought they had reached the main road out of Niort, they found themselves taken on yet another circuitous stretch of buildings and tree-lined avenues. In the end, Toby found it easier to concentrate on listening to Frances' intermittent instructions such as "junction coming up, turn right." Or, "signal right, Toby, *now*!" And soon they were on the final run heading for La Rochelle.

Frances settled back and got Toby's iPod out of the glove compartment, much as Claudia had done at the start of the trip on the previous day.

"I see you've got quite a bit of classical stuff on here as well as contemporary," she remarked.

He told her briefly about the types of classical music he preferred, and then suggested she page through the playlist marked 'Top 100' if she wanted to see his favourites in pop and rock.

"Let me know if you see anything at all which might be on yours – I'd be interested. There's a real mix of stuff there. We all like to think our choices will be shared by others, but of course it never works out like that. And why should it?"

She grunted her agreement and said: "Hush, I'm trying to concentrate!" and carried on looking. Every so often she muttered things like "OK", "fair enough", "uh-huh", "well, alright" and "hmm, interesting". Toby hoped she was being polite by refraining from negative exclamations like: "not in a million years!", "yuck!", "you've got to be kidding!" and similar.

They were well on the road when Frances asked him:

"Are you going to be OK on your own for the next fortnight? What's it going to be like, where you're going?"

"Well, I'm looking forward to it, if that's what you mean. Of course it'll be a first time so I don't know *exactly* what it's going to be like or what I'll find there. But it's like I told you that evening in the pub when we met again for the first time in months: I've done my research and read up about the island. And all the pictures I've seen on the web-sites make it look pretty attractive – interesting, certainly. There's real 17th century history in the main town, a ruined priory somewhere, more than one decent church to look at; there are the remains of German WW2 bunkers on several beaches. And then there's the prospect of being able to cycle everywhere at a traffic-free leisurely pace – that sounds appealing. Shall I go on?"

He paused, thinking. After a moment he continued:

"I mean, in a way it's a pity you can't come too – you might like it, and I think there could be room. But obviously you can't because of course you're on your own holiday to the Dordogne right now with every prospect of having a great time there. You can tell me all about it when we're back home; I shall be very interested to hear. Wouldn't mind going down there myself one day, so your report could be crucial!"

He grinned at her.

"No, like I said, I'm good with my own company, and if you were going somewhere new with someone else, you'd need to be jolly careful in choosing who you went with. You can't invite just anyone. And they've got to like you too."

He trailed off, realising that he was straying into uncertain waters. Mustn't give her the wrong idea. After all, we're just friends, right?

"Of course, you're right," she agreed. "You can't just go with anyone. Girls like to go with friends – that's natural. It's the men who tend to be the loners. Still, friends can be very useful sometimes. As friends. You might try it sometime."

Was this sarcasm? Or was it a verbal dig at him, he wondered? Deciding that it was the latter, he was quick to thank her for her "invaluable" contribution helping him to navigate some tricky parts of the long route.

"You're not being patronising, are you, by any chance?"

"No," Toby replied hastily. "I mean it. You're obviously very good at spotting things quickly, and you've been so calm about it. You've made it much easier for me to find the way, especially when I've needed to concentrate on the road itself all the time. I don't know how many times I would have gone round those roundabouts if I'd been on my own – probably still be doing it now!" he joked.

"Thanks," she said, smiling at him. "It's always nice to be appreciated honestly."

They lapsed into an easy silence. She turned round to check on Claudia who was still quiet in the back of the car.

A short while later, Toby said: "Nearly there. Look, you can see the outskirts of La Rochelle ahead in the distance."

And not long after, they swung off the N11 and very soon reached the airport turn-off. He found a convenient place to drop them off a few yards up the approach road so that he didn't have to pay to go in the car-park.

"I'll wait here with your cases while you two go off and get your hire-car. Bring it back here and we can transfer all your stuff quickly, and you can be on your way. How's the head, Claude?"

"Much better now, thanks for asking – I think I caught it just in time." She beamed him a big smile.

He waited for the best part of half an hour before a Renault Clio drew up beside his car and the girls got out.

"Looks good," he said.

Within 5 minutes, their bags were in the Clio and they were saying goodbye. Claudia was back to her normal bouncy self.

"Thanks *so* much, Toby. You've been great, really great. It's been a good trip, and thanks for planning such an interesting route. Have a good holiday." And she gave him a huge hug and another big kiss on the mouth. "Come on, Fran, let's get going!" She hurried to get into their car.

"Just let me say goodbye to Toby," Frances called. She turned to Toby.

"Yes, thanks again for everything. For getting us here safely. And for being so nice," she added.

He suddenly felt he was about to lose her. Stupid!

This is the start of *your* holiday, he told himself firmly. Sure, she's being nice right now but let her go, she's got her own life to lead. Still, he hadn't bargained that he might feel quite like this towards her.

"Stay in touch, will you?" he asked. "And phone or text me to let me know when you get the car back to the airport next week so I know you made it safely?" He held her shoulders for a moment.

She moved into him and made to kiss him – and then checked and drew back uncertainly, unsure of herself. Instead, she said quietly: "Yes, I promise."

"Don't you forget now. That's a definite promise?"

"Sure."

"Come on, Fran. Don't take all day! Hurry up!" yelled Claudia from inside the car.

Frances reached up to stroke his cheek briefly, gave him one more gentle smile, and "Got to go. Can't keep the Boss waiting!" she said ruefully. And turned and got in the car.

"Good luck!" he called after them.

He waved them off until they were out of sight, then climbed back into the driver's seat, breathed a sigh, and headed in the opposite direction to the Pont de Ré and the island.

Chapter Twelve

Toby's holiday – Part 1: Toby

Within just a few minutes he reached the toll booths for the crossing, and when he topped the long graceful bridge and saw the island stretching away in front of him, any lingering thoughts of Frances went clean out of the window. He gasped inwardly at the view which immediately seemed to offer him the prospect of excitement and new interest. Once over the bridge, he followed the directions to the main town, St Martin, where he found signs which took him on to his destination, Le Bois Plage. Easy enough, but it then took him another 10 minutes to find a way to drive to the studio he had rented. He found all the one-way streets confusing but in the end he arrived in the centre of the village, with the studio just a couple of streets away from the church.

He was soon unpacking the car and installing himself; it really didn't take long! Once inside, he found that the living room area included a single bed/divan as well as a table, chairs and a small armchair. He went straight into the bedroom. A good-sized double-bed to stretch out in – nice!

And he was glad that he had remembered to bring a couple of sheets and a pillowcase from home – bedding was not among the first things he wanted to be buying.

But food was! Back in the living room, he found the folder of local information and saw that there was a choice of large supermarkets but he'd have to drive up to St Martin to find them and stock up for the first week at least. This would also allow him to become more familiar with the local geography straightaway. He remembered seeing an Intermarché supermarket on the way, so his first priority would be to find his way back there to get the groceries.

While he was settling in, he checked the drawers of kitchen cutlery to see if he needed to buy basic equipment like a tin opener or cheese grater. The cooker was electric so he had no need of matches. The food cupboards were entirely bare of course, so he knew he would have to include basics like salt and pepper on the list. The rest he would play by ear when he got to the supermarket.

He brought his iPod in from the car, and opened up his laptop to register the studio's wi-fi code. He searched for a convenient wall plug for recharging the battery later and then realised he'd need an adaptor for the European 2-pin system.

Damn! He'd have to hope that he could get one of those universal adaptors from the supermarket, one which could accept the British square-pin plugs. Add it to the list. Focussing on the laptop brought Frances to mind. He thought he would establish contact by e-mail in case she needed to get in touch with him for any reason, knowing that she'd be able to pick up any messages on her mobile phone.

A little over an hour later, he arrived back in the car loaded with food and wine. Having unpacked, he opened all the windows, set up his iPod and speakers, selected a playlist, opened his first bottle of Rosé, and cooked himself a light supper. He followed this with a leisurely stroll down to the nearest beach – he found it didn't take much over 10 minutes.

He sat on the sand for a while simply contemplating the sea and the overall peace of the place before returning to the studio to sit and read outside in the warm evening air, glass of wine in hand and the bottle on the table. With the light beginning to fade, he went inside and unfolded the map of the island which he had bought at the supermarket. I'll drive to the far end of the island tomorrow, he decided. Take my bathers and sample one or two of the beaches on that side. Find somewhere for lunch, or come back here. Savouring the novelty of it all and the sense of freedom of choice, he went to bed a happy man.

On the following day, he got up at a leisurely hour and had a late breakfast, after which he put together enough things for an outing. He soon found out how relatively small the island was if you were going everywhere by car. Round at the far end of the island, he found a good beach for bathing and relaxing, and there was some evidence of ruined WW2 machine-gun posts now fallen into the sand. He supposed that, with the beach facing the mainland, it would not have needed as strong a defence against invasion as the Atlantic-facing coastline. After an hour or so he drove back down the coast to the western end of the island. He found a much longer, wider, beach facing out to sea. Sure enough, he found the remains of impressive major concrete bunkers which would have housed much larger cannon with a far longer range. They were all adorned with graffiti, some of which was highly artistic and, he thought, worthy of a place in any exhibition of student art. He photographed anything that appealed and then had another bathe in the sea.

Later, on the way home, he remembered that he'd spotted the island's main lighthouse, so made the small diversion to check it out. Its tower rose tall, majestic, imposing, and was unexpectedly octagonal. The topless stalk of its predecessor stood forlornly closer to the shoreline. On the seaward side, all sand had disappeared, replaced by rock shelving which at low tide extended far out to sea, taking the eye way out to what must have been the original lighthouse, though whether this was long-abandoned or still somehow in use, he couldn't tell. More photographs of past and present edifices, and he was off returning home.

Driving through the township of La Couarde, he turned off the main street, following a sign to one of the beaches. Nice, he thought, but I've swum enough for one day. Must hire a bike tomorrow and cycle over here. See how many different beaches I can find to swim off. The tide was still out and he could see where underwater rocks were exposed. Must see if there's a tide table in the house, he reminded himself – or else buy one in the village.

Back at the studio and finding none, he decided to stave off his hunger and walk round the corner into the village centre. There might well be a small supermarket still open and, anyway, he needed to check out bicycle hire. The information folder showed that he had quite a choice of suppliers for that. A few minutes later, he had reached the market square and the shops and, sure enough, there was a small Carrefour. Being Sunday afternoon it was closed but at least it was available; it would be useful later in the week for restocking the odd items but also, he realised, for getting daily baguettes.

Across the road he saw a newsagent which surely would sell tide-tables, wouldn't it? It was also closed but, no matter, there was always tomorrow, he said to himself. And then, on the way back, he realised that he could probably get the information via the internet. Either way, he should be covered. He reminded himself that he would be staying for a fortnight, so would be subject to different tides, including the outgoing tides when any rocks would be just under the surface. OK, he thought, must look for some cheap beach shoes for swimming in. One more thing for tomorrow.

The next morning, he walked back into the village centre and to a couple of small bike-hire shops to get the best quote for twelve days, which would cover him up to the last full day of his fortnight. He chose the hirer nearest to his route back to the studio, concluded his business, and walked away with his metal steed, past the church and down to the Carrefour where he bought his baguette and, luckily, a pair of swim-shoes in the right size. He cycled back to the house and put together a picnic lunch. He'd brought his old hiking backpack from home so could carry his food, book, iPod and earphones, and other small items in it, and use the bike's pannier to carry his bathers, towel and a beach-mat he'd found in the house.

All set? Perfect! Get out the map of dedicated cycle routes and plan an outing to ……. ah! to Loix, over there, straight across the island. Not too far for a first day, and I see I can take a longer and more circuitous route if I cycle up to the edge of St Martin first and then turn left along the top coastline. I can come back a different route, down to La Couarde, and check out that beach again. Probably need a swim after that! Yes, that looks good.

And off he went. The cycle paths were easy to follow, once he had got out of the village, and he had no trouble finding his way. He was tremendously impressed by the fortifications around St Martin, which he guessed were 17th century. They had all the look of the great military engineer Vauban about them – he must check that out as soon as he got home later. Further on, he found he was approaching Loix on a charming causeway above the salt marshes, leading to sluice gates on the edge of the village. Across these and cycling on to the centre, he found the church and was amused to see that its forecourt was not ecclesiastical but was actually the village pétanque pitch. Right in front of it! Hopefully there'd be no games or matches in progress when the worshippers came out after a church service! Then into the square, where he found a café for a cup of coffee and a pastry, and sat watching the world around him. He was having another excellent day.

Excited by the fortifications he had seen at St Martin, he cycled up there on the Tuesday morning. He could see that they were extensive round the landward side of the town and, once inside the old walls, he found that the seaward side was equally well buttressed – clearly this town would have been well-defended in the Sun King's reign. The town was built at the top of rising ground which, inside the fortifications, sloped down to the harbour. Here all the moorings seemed to him to be completely given over to privately-owned yachts and launches. There was little or no sign of any commercial shipping. With possibly a couple of exceptions, every single establishment along the harbour front seemed to be a restaurant.

He could see the top of the town church tower above the buildings so walked his bike up a couple of side streets to go and have a look inside. From the outside, the church did not look so very big, but inside the impression was of a vast space – was this a trick of perspective, he wondered? Around the church were various boards recording historical facts about the church, the town and the island. He found the accounts of events during the Revolution particularly interesting, as were those about the storm damage which left the original tower in ruins.

Emerging from the church, he explored the back streets, cycling out to the coastal fortifications on the far side, and past what looked as if it might have once been a large naval barracks subsequently converted into a prison. He decided to explore a little further beyond the town walls and soon found himself in a car park next to a small beach where the tide was fortunately in. Time to stop, have a break, sit on the beach, and maybe a swim too.

Later, he cycled back to the studio, enjoying the leisurely pace along with the challenge of finding his way through the maze of narrow side streets on the edge of the village. Only a couple of wrong turnings this time and, anyway, his good sense of direction ensured that he would get back to the centre of the village in the end. He fixed himself a late lunch-time snack and then settled down for the rest of the afternoon to relax. He dozed off in the sunshine. He dreamed of a giant lighthouse where he was the eye of the light, able to scan and search right to the very horizon; and there were mermaids unaccountably living in caves like troglodytes who were painting the floors, not the walls, in great splashes of random patterns and colours which strongly reminded him of a Jackson Pollock!

When he woke up, he had an idea of e-mailing Frances. Just something to establish contact, he told himself. She'd have her phone of course, but he didn't expect a reply. He kept the message brief.

> "Hi F. Hope all going well for you both. Good weather, caves, etc. Having good time – pity you can't be here too. Cycling everywhere at a gentle pace feels very liberating. Warm weather, good beaches, good bathing. St Martin really interesting, except too many restaurants for choice! Off to

find a medieval market and the
ruined abbey tomorrow. Have
fun. Love. T."

He thought he could get away with signing off
like that – nice and casual, nothing in it really. He
pressed Send, then poured another glass of wine
and returned to his book. In only three days he felt
he had really caught the tempo of things and was
getting to grips with the place. More exploring
tomorrow.

Accordingly the next morning, he prepared the
usual picnic lunch, packed up and set off through
the village to follow the cycle path which would
take him past the local sports stadium and on
down the long hill to the small town of La Flotte
where, the tourist information indicated, he
should find a medieval market. Did that mean he
would see a whole load of people dressed up in
medieval costume selling things from a pretend
market? When he got there, he found a standard
market but housed in a walled courtyard which,
from the age of the wooden beams surrounding
it, looked authentically old. It was crowded, as a
local market should be – not a sign of tourist hype
anywhere, although a few of the stalls had the
look of trying to attract the late holidaymaker. He

came out and made his way across to the harbour – another mini marina – and treated himself to an ice-cream. He saw a couple of bistros amongst the restaurants and strolled over to check the menus for future reference.

A short ride took him through harvested cornfields where the last of the summer wildflowers were still around: poppies contrasting with the dark purple of the tufted vetch and deep pinkish-mauve of the mallow flowers beside the cycle path. He came up to the ruins referred to as a priory, although he had read that it had started life in the 11th century as a Cistercian abbey which had fallen into disuse and decay in the 17th century. It was small, but had a charm about it in the sunshine, surrounded as it was by cornfields. And the shelter of its walls offered a pleasant place to stop and have his lunch.

Afterwards he saddled up and cycled further along the cliff path until he came to a small fortification – another star fort. Although he found it closed, the information board told him that it had been built in 1625 which he knew from his history was two years before the invasion by the English under the Duke of Buckingham trying to bring aid to the Huguenots. Apparently Buckingham had ignored the fort, to his ultimate cost.

Toby read on, and then photographed what he could from outside the gates, before cycling back to La Flotte and its small beach. Time for a swim before he returned home.

He decided to make Thursday a 'rest day' from excursions, and satisfied himself with riding back to St Martin and the church, so that he could pay the small fee and go up the church tower. As he expected, he got great views for miles around from the top, including being able to look down on the rooves of all the houses surrounding the church. He tried to spot the places he had been to so far, and was surprised to find that the view did not extend southward as far as Le Bois Plage which, after all, was only a couple of miles directly across the island. Maybe the tower wasn't as high as it had looked from the ground?

He returned home for some lunch and spent the bulk of the afternoon relaxing on his nearest beach. With the tide already on the way out, he was glad of his swim-shoes when he went in for a bathe. That evening, he sent another e-mail to Frances, telling her what he had done since Tuesday and wishing her a good journey home on the Saturday. He turned his attention to his next excursion for tomorrow, and decided it was time to strike out and cycle much further afield.

And so the next morning saw him set off across the fields and vineyards on the long route to the town of Ars which was on the way to the lighthouse. A good north-westerly breeze had blown up not long after starting, and by the time he reached the salt-pan flats on the way, he was having to pedal quite hard against the strength of the wind. By then he knew he was going in the right direction because he could see quite clearly across the pans the spire of the church at Ars which looked like a space rocket waiting to be launched. It was most unusual. The closer he got, the more he realised that the top half of the spire had been painted black – why, he had no idea, but it stood out quite clearly, so maybe that was part of the reason?

By the time he had reached the small harbour, there was much more shelter from the stiff breeze. He consulted his map and deliberated where he should aim for lunch. Should he explore up beside the river channel taking the boats out to sea? He did not want to cycle as far as the lighthouse because he had been there already. Equally, he wasn't all that keen on cycling on as far as the large nature reserve. In the end he decided to cycle onwards through the town and strike across the fields to try and find a cosy sheltered spot out of the wind in the wooded dunes above the shoreline. This took him a further half hour but after a couple of false paths off the road, he finally found what he was looking for. And by the time he had finished his food and had a quiet snooze under the trees, the breeze had quietened down.

As he headed back to Le Bois Plage, he soon realised that now he had the wind behind him, so that the ride back was far less strenuous, and so more enjoyable. By the time he got back home, the breeze had dropped to almost nothing, so he turned round and cycled back to the beach at La Couarde, to spend the rest of the afternoon on the sand. And in the sea.

Yes, life was still being very good to him.

Chapter Thirteen

Toby's holiday – Part 2: A Friendly Guest

Saturday dawned, and Toby realised two things: he had been here a whole week and was now halfway through his holiday, and he had not yet spent any time looking round Le Bois Plage village where he was staying. After breakfast, he checked his e-mails and his phone for any texts in from Frances but there was nothing. Slightly disappointed, he still hoped he would get some message from her, however brief, at some point during the day, letting him know that she and Claudia had reached the airport safely and were on their way home. Then he put that to the back of his mind and strolled into the centre of the village.

The market was bustling, and this market wasn't so much for fruit and veg as for everything else! There were even roundabouts for the children. Through the market on the far side beyond the church there were more proper shops. So he spent a happy morning just mooching around the place; he bought a couple of cheap t-shirts, had a look inside the church, and ended up in the Carrefour buying a few things. And some more wine.

He strolled back to the studio and prepared a light lunch. He had just finished clearing up after it when his phone announced that a text had come through. That'll be Frances or Claude presumably, he thought. The text was, sure enough, from Frances and its message was as he expected. It read: "At LR airport now. X. F." All well then. Pity she didn't say any more, but at least she's done what she promised. He texted back: "Thanks. Hope all well. Have good trip. See you in Blighty." He was in no hurry, he had the whole afternoon unplanned. What should he do? He'd read in the information folder that there was a recommended restaurant just a few roads away. He'd cycle over and check out their menu and prices.

This didn't take long and, satisfied, he rode back to the studio where he poured himself a fresh glass of wine and settled down with his book and his music in the afternoon sun. About an hour later, he was just beginning to doze off when a second text from Frances came through. That's nice, he thought; probably saying goodbye before they start boarding.

But this time the message was definitely not as expected. It read: "Claude boarding. Me not. Problem. Please come to airport asap." Oh, what's she gone and done now? he moaned. Not on the plane with Claudia? Wasn't she all booked up for the flight back? What sort of problem? Hell! I'd better get over there straightaway. Now where's some money for the bridge toll on the way back? Drat the girl! He texted back: "Am on way now. Hold on."

Within minutes he was in the car and away back up the road towards the bridge off the island. It took him about 20 minutes to reach the airport turn-off. He drove up and parked on the same spot on the approach road where he had dropped the girls a week ago, and sprinted up to the terminal building. There was Frances sitting beside her case and bags. She was watching out for him and stood up as he reached her. She threw herself at him and gave him a huge hug, a kiss on the cheek, and a broad smile.

Worried, he held her away from him and garbled:

"What? Why are you still here? Why aren't you on the plane with Claude? What on earth is the problem you texted about? Are you alright? Are you hurt? What's the matter?"

"Whoa, whoa, not so fast! Too many questions all at once. Aren't you at all pleased to see me?"

He held her arms.

"Of course I am! But that doesn't answer the question. Any of them! You need to explain."

"I will, but in the car, not out here. Help me get my bags to the car will you? Please?"

"But you'll miss your flight!"

"Oh, I've missed that already – at least, it's too late to get to Boarding now. Look, let me explain in the car. Please, Toby."

Reluctantly, and still mystified, he hefted her case and carried it down the road, to stow it away in the back, by which time Frances was already in the car. He got in.

"We can't stay parked here, Frances, and I'm guessing your explanations are going to take a little time, yes? Look, I'll drive back down the road and see if I can find a pull-in where we can talk."

"Thank you," she said politely and put her hand on his for a moment. She was relieved that he didn't immediately recoil and snatch it away, which meant that he wasn't angry at her. Yet.

He soon found a place where he could safely pull off the road and park.

"Now," he said, turning to her. "Just what is all this about? What's happened? How can I help?"

"Thank you for offering your help before I've even explained. I always knew you were kind. Now, before I say anything, can you promise not to get mad at me?"

"As bad as that, is it? Just what *have* you done?" He looked pointedly at her. "Alright, I suppose I can but try," he said, half-grudgingly. "So, shoot."

"Well …..," she began.

"Hang on!," Toby interrupted. "Where's your flight ticket ? What happened to it?"

"I haven't got one,"

"What? How can you not have a plane ticket to get home?"

"I didn't buy one. Toby, shut up a minute. I'm trying to explain."

"Sorry," he replied meekly. "Please go on."

"Thank *you*! Now, think back. How many times already have you all-but invited me to come and join you here? "It's a pity you can't come too – you might like it, and I think there would be room," you said. Well, I don't know if you really have got room for a guest, but I'm willing to take that chance. So I'd like to take you up on your kind offer, however you might have wrapped it up in your funny obscure way. I remember telling you, I'd actually booked a normal fortnight's holiday leave but hadn't decided on the second week."

She continued:

"And the more you told me about where you were going and what you hoped it would be like, the more appealing it all sounded and the more interested I became. After all, I'm here to experience as much of France as I can. And then your two e-mails arrived and I thought: I want to be with him, there. So I discussed it with Claude and she said if that's what I wanted then I should go for it. So here I am. May I come and stay with you for this week and travel home with you next weekend? Please?"

She turned the charm up to max. and gave him the most appealing look she could.

The whole situation was taking him quite by surprise. Once again she had hit him with something totally unexpected. Like a typical man he played for time while he thought it through, and sought refuge in considering the practical implications of her request.

"OK. Well, the place *is* small, there's no denying. But there's a separate bed in the sitting room area, away from the bedroom, where you could sleep. We'd need to buy bed sheets for you but that'd be easy, and pretty cheap at one of the supermarkets. You'd need to hire a bicycle for a few days if you're going to experience the island properly, but I guess you're already saving on the cost of the flight. Oh, and I warn you, I like to bathe in the sea at least once every day – I'm trying to see just how many different beaches I can find to swim off. It'd be no good if you're one of those girls who just likes to lie on the sand sunbathing all day and who never goes in the water."

"No, I brought my bathers with me, and we both got to swim in a river a couple of times during the week," she assured him. "And we'd share the cost of food, of course," she said eagerly, as she saw him sounding as if he was already weakening. "I'll bet you've been living quite frugally – and this is France, after all!

"Living healthily, I like to think!" he replied, pretending to be mildly affronted. He found he was coming round to the idea somewhat quicker than expected, and was almost surprised to realise that he wasn't objecting. In fact, he *was* glad to see her and it could be fun showing her the places that he'd found. Perhaps he could put her own personal history behind him? And, he told himself, we're pretty easy in each other's company, so it might work. And if it doesn't, it's only for a week – surely I can last that long?

"Please, Toby. Say yes? Look, it's only for a week, and if it doesn't work, well, it won't be the end of the world, will it?" But if he says yes, then I'll jolly well do my best to make it work for both of us, she thought. I just don't believe he could be *that* awful.

"Please don't think I'm blackmailing you but, if you say no, well, I'll have to stay with you until I can book the next flight home, which might well be days away. But I'd rather be with you properly and not have to worry about that. Toby, would you be prepared to share the rest of your holiday with a friend who happens to be me?"

He looked at her steadily and made up his mind. "Alright. Let's see if we can spend a companionable week together. But we must agree right from the start not to fight, and to work out how we can find common ground when we disagree. I'm not having my holiday spoiled by sulks or moods or harsh words, and I guess you don't want that either." He had a thought, and brightened up. "There's already lots I've found that I'd like to show you. Yes - in fact, thinking about it, I'd rather like to share it all with you." He reached over and squeezed her hand encouragingly before starting up the car and heading down to the motorway and back to the Bridge Tolls.

"Get a load of this bridge and this view!" he said proudly as they crossed over the turquoise strait separating the island from the mainland. Wow, he had been here only a week and already he felt proud to show off the place, the island he had discovered.

"We'll go home first so you can unload your things. Then we'll measure the spare bed so we can get the right size of sheet, make a food shopping list, and drive up to one of the supermarkets at St Martin. We'll organise bike hire for you tomorrow – it's already too late today. Yep, I think you're really going to like this place."

She saw how excited he was now sounding, which gave her a lift and made her feel so much better about deciding to stay in France for a while longer. And his excitement was infectious; she found herself looking forward already to she knew not what, but she trusted him and so knew she was happy to give it a go.

They spent the rest of the day much as he had done when he arrived the week before. They made a basic shopping list, knowing that they would undoubtedly see much more to pick up when they were trolleying around the supermarket. The groceries done, including the bedding, they returned to the studio to make up a bed for Frances and to give her a chance to unpack her bags and settle in while he unpacked the shopping. Then they took the car down to the nearest beach and sat for a long time, chatting easily as if they had both been together all week.

Eventually, with the daylight already turning to dusk, they drove back and cooked their supper. Surprisingly, for a small studio, there was enough room in the kitchen area for both of them to move and work around each other. Initially there was an awful lot of "Sorry" and "Excuse me" from both of them, but the meal was achieved with no major upsets, and was pronounced a success for a first effort together. The studio had a small garden area and, the evening being warm, they sat outside with their coffee until Frances declared she really did need to go to bed; it had been quite a tiring day, after all.

Toby realised that, because of the separate sleeping arrangements and now having to share the facilities, they'd need to turn in at the same time. "Let me go through the bathroom first," he said, "and I'll take myself out of your way and undress in the bedroom. You can then have the run of the place and take your time getting yourself to bed. Pop your head round the door and say Goodnight when you're ready."

She thanked him and waited until he had gone into the bedroom. Inevitably it took her a little while to get used to where things were but in the end she finished her toilet quickly, knocked on his door to say goodnight, and retired to her own bed.

The following morning, Toby woke up to see another bright day outside. He remembered his 'guest' in the living room and thought he'd better check up on her. She might be one of those people who appreciates an early morning cup of tea before they get up, he thought. So he made sure he was respectable before leaving the bedroom. Frances was awake but still in bed. He offered her a cup of tea, which she accepted. As the kettle was boiling he asked: "And how did you sleep last night? Was it alright?"

"Not too bad," she answered, "although it could have been a lot better. It took me a long time to get to sleep, and then I woke up several times during the night. Got back to sleep again each time, though."

"Sorry about that," replied Toby. "Getting used to a strange bed in unusual circumstances, I expect. Hopefully you'll have a better night tonight."

"Let's hope so. OK if you're first through the bathroom while I drink my tea?"

"Sure," he said. "Good idea. Then I can get breakfast ready while you're in there. Cereal followed by toast and jam or the remains of last night's baguette OK for you?"

"Sounds reasonable," she returned.

"Coffee or more tea, when you're ready?"

"I'll move on to coffee, I think, please. But wait until I'm out, will you?"

"Of course, m'lady. It shall be as you desire!" He bowed to her ceremoniously.

Breakfast over, they walked his bike into the village centre to the same hire shop as before, and they got a small discount for 'repeat business', although more probably because the main French holidays were already over and there was less business around. Thence to the Carrefour to get a fresh baguette for lunch, and back to the house to plan their first outing together.

"So where would you like to show me first? Shall we do a gentle ride to start with, so I can get used to the whole thing?"

"OK," said Toby. "So I think we'll do the circuit I did on my first proper outing and head for Loix." He showed her the route on the cycle map. "We can stop there for a bit of a break and have coffee and stuff – if you'd like to, I mean. And then if we cycle a bit further out of the village, we could head for the nearest beach, there." He pointed on the map. "I suggest we have lunch and stay and relax there for a while, assuming the weather stays reasonable. It's not a terribly long ride back either, so we can come home during the afternoon and decide if we want to stop there or go down to the beach and have a swim perhaps. Work up a bit of an appetite before supper, for example."

"I'm in your hands," said Frances. "Treat me gently, Sir – it's only my first day!" She giggled. "No, it's OK. I'm keen to see everything you've discovered which you think I'd like."

"That's the idea!" replied Toby. "Come on, let's get going." He led the way through the twist of streets until he struck the cycle path up to St

Martin. He skirted the town as before and carried on in front until they were about half-way to Loix. He came to a halt and waited for her to come alongside. "The cycle path is very clear from here onwards, so why don't you go in front and I'll call out directions if I need to. Then if you want to stop for any reason, like checking a bird or a view, you can and I'll be behind you and won't go sailing on ahead without knowing."

"Thanks, I'd like that. But catch up if I stop in case I need to ask you anything, OK?"

For Toby, this meant that he had to cycle more slowly than he would have liked, but the upside was, he soon realised, that he could enjoy the shapely upright back view of the girl in front of him. An unexpected bonus!

The further the day wore on, the more pleased he was about his decision to let her stay. So far, things had worked out well, but it was still early days and, presumably, things could turn against him just as easily as carrying on as they were at present. She was still quite an unknown quantity, after all. And look at it from her side. It must be the same for her, and she was the one who had, as it were, crashed his holiday, so she must be feeling uncertain about him and his reaction to her presence. OK, he told himself. Be careful and be nice. Make her feel welcome and accepted. Remember that it's her holiday too.

So over their picnic lunch, he did his best to keep the conversation light and uncontentious. She declined his offer to join him in the water when the tide had come back up the beach sufficiently for a swim. Or maybe it was a question of confidence in front of him? He guessed she would be watching him from the beach, assessing him, but he wasn't out to make an impression so he bathed leisurely as if she wasn't there. She must have been encouraged because, when they finally got back to the studio, she declared: "Let's carry on down to the nearest beach. I want to swim. You coming?" She dashed inside, got her bathers and went into the bedroom to change while he waited for her outside. She grabbed her towel and ran out. "Hurry up!" she grinned.

His own swimming shorts were still wet from his earlier dip but he agreed to go with her. It took him a while to struggle back into them, so she had been in the water some minutes before he joined her. He observed how tidily she swam, each arm stretching lazily but precisely forward and gliding smoothly through the water in front. He found himself envying such graceful ease.

Not that he was a bad swimmer himself but he knew his crawl splashed more than it should, so he confined himself to gentle breast stroke near her but not close up. She smiled a lot at him so was obviously enjoying herself.

He noticed that she tended to stop after about eight strokes - she evidently wasn't a strong swimmer. Anyway, she hadn't the shoulders for it, he saw. He was relieved. This sort of swimming was similar to his own standard, and the last thing he wanted was for things to develop into a competition between them. She also showed that she wasn't one for staying in the water for long. Having satisfied herself for a first dip, she waved to him and called out: "I'm going out now – my shoulders are starting to get cold." He let her go on ahead back up the beach and stayed in the water for another five minutes or so before coming out, by which time she had towelled down and changed back into her clothes.

"Good?" he grinned at her cheerfully.

"Good!" she responded, "but not for long. I could do with a warm drink so let's not hang around now. Get yourself dry quickly and we can get back to the house."

"Yes, m'm," said Toby and knuckled his forehead.

"Glad to see you haven't forgotten your place, Chivers!" She showed she remembered the banter they had had months ago on the way to the restaurant on his birthday.

"Absolutely not, Mistress, no!" came the servile reply, in the same voice as before. And they both giggled, just as they had done before.

The next day, over breakfast, Toby asked solicitously after her night's sleep.

"Not wonderfully better, I'm afraid," replied Frances. "Which is stupid really. You'd think, after sharing a double bed with Claude for the best part of a week, I'd be glad to be back on my own."

"Right, that settles it," said Toby firmly. "We'll change rooms. I'll move my stuff out of the bedroom and you can move in. It's a decent double bed so hopefully you'll get a good night's sleep from now on."

"No, I can't do that," she protested. "I can't turf you out of your room. I'm the guest, remember – not supposed to be here. What'll you do?"

"Easy. I can sleep in a single bed just the same. And, look, I'm only being selfish. The more bad nights you have, the crabbier you'll feel each day, and that'll spoil things for both of us."

"Just a sec," she interjected. "How would *you* know? How many women have you slept with to sound so sure?"

"What? No. Well, it stands to reason, surely. Everyone gets grumpy through a lack of proper sleep. Don't they?"

"I suppose so," she conceded.

"Well then," Toby continued. "So no arguments; that's what we're going to do! We'll do the swap this evening. Anyway, it's far more appropriate for the lady to have the private room, so everything will be socially correct!"

"What tosh you do talk sometimes!" she said but smiled at him gratefully. "Thank you for being a brick about it, as Claude would say."

"Ah, Claude, where is she now?" He was not being serious.

"Back at work, no doubt, and frankly I couldn't care. We had an OK time together, don't get me wrong. But I'm happier here with you." She looked at him and gave him a grin. "At least so far!" she teased.

"Point taken!," Toby grinned. "Now get a shift on,

you. I want to show you the so-called medieval market and the ruined abbey. It'll be about the same distance as yesterday but it'll be a bit harder pedalling as you've got a couple of hills to cycle up."

She pulled a face but said bravely: "I'll manage it." And then realised he was pulling her leg. "Hang on. You told me this island was flat so where are these hills suddenly coming into it?"

"OK, OK. Just teasing. Sorry. No, let's call them "long slopes" then – that would be much more accurate. Nothing a champion swimmer of your calibre can't handle with ease!"

"What's that about my swimming? Have you been peeking, you old Tom?"

"No, no, honest, guv'. Don't be angry wiv' me – I jus' happen'd to be passin' and saw you in the wa'er!" He put on a stage whine. Then, in his normal voice: "No, you just looked very nice, that's all. Very graceful style, I thought."

"OK, I'll let you off this time," she pretended to glare, but showed she'd taken the compliment. "But those "long slopes"? Nothing too arduous, I hope?"

"No, really. You'll be fine. They're easy in a lower gear, so no need to get excited."

"OK, let's be off soon. Anywhere we can stop for a bit of lunch on the way?"

"Well, instead of taking a picnic, we could stop in La Flotte and have something at a café or bistro on the harbour. I think I saw one or two last week."

"That sounds nice. Let's do that."

The rest of the day passed pleasantly. Frances liked the market because of all the different stalls and produce there, and then was charmed by the abbey/priory. "A bit on the small side," was her comment, "but after all it's a relatively small island and it was probably a large part of the community back in its prime."

That evening, after swapping rooms and having had supper, they sat down at the table with their coffee and Toby got out a double pack of cards. "Fancy a game of something? What do you play?"

"What had you in mind?" replied Frances diplomatically.

"Well, how about I teach you how to play 'Spite & Malice' – unless you know it already, that is. It's not particularly well known, not like whist and all of its trick-taking derivatives."

"No, not one I've heard of. How do you play it?"

Toby explained that it was basically a race to be the first to get rid of all the cards in your 13-card stock, by playing out of your hand of 5 cards. He explained the few rules. "And Kings and Jokers are wild," he added. "I was taught this game by my aged grandparents when I was about 8 or 9 years old. They came up from London to live with us in their last years."

"So about the time we were in class together," commented Frances.

"Yes, I guess so. Pity I didn't pass it on to you at the time!" he grinned.

"You didn't like me very much back then, remember? You and the rest of the class," she added, a touch bitterly.

"I know, I know. I still squirm a bit when I think about it. But, come on, that's just the way we were then. We boys just thought of girls as weak and soppy versions of ourselves, so pretty much a waste of space for anything worthwhile. It wasn't abnormal. It was just that it was no fun at all for you." He paused, still feeling a twinge of guilt from the memory. "But," he quickly added, "I came to your rescue that time, didn't I? So I can't have been all bad, can I? And look how it's turned out all these years later. We're here together!"

"Yes you did, and you seem to have turned out alright. On balance! Now, let's get on with this game."

She quickly got the hang of it after a couple of trial rounds, and soon was taking great delight in 'spiting' him whenever she could by stopping him from using the cards from his own stock when it was his turn. Time passed, and it wasn't so long before she announced that she'd like to make a hot drink and retire early-ish so as to get a good night's sleep at last.

"Shall I make you one too?"

"No thanks. I'll just sit here and read a bit while you get to bed, and then follow you in the bathroom."

Not long afterwards, she said Goodnight, took her drink into the bedroom and closed the door.

Another good day, he thought, as he switched off the lights and got into bed.

The weather still held the next day, though there was general light cloud and a bit of a breeze. He asked Frances if she was up for a longer cycle ride, over to Ars with the space rocket for a church tower. That sounds intriguing, came the reply. And, because she had had a good night's sleep at last, declared she was feeling up for the challenge.

"If you find it feels like we're cycling into wind on the way, and it might," he said, remembering his ride the previous week, "you can take comfort in the fact that you'll have it pushing you nicely along on the way back!"

"Fair enough. Let's do it!" she said gamely.

On the way, she was particularly struck by the number of open vineyards they cycled past.

"This cycle path we're on at the moment is so long and straight, it makes me think of all those old disused railway track-beds back home which got turned into walking and cycle paths," she observed.

Toby wondered if she'd accidentally hit on a truth and determined to look on the internet sometime to see if there once had been a small railway on the island. Indeed, when they reached the harbour at Ars, something he hadn't noticed previously, there was a building alongside a small car park which looked for all the world like it could have been a French railway station building. He was more interested than Frances, but she observed quite reasonably that it would make sense for there to have been a railway and some sort of station at the harbour, to pick up stuff delivered to the quayside by working boats.

By the time they got back to Le Bois Plage, she was tired and a bit saddle-sore. Toby suggested that they make a last bit of effort, collect their bathers and cycle the short distance to the beach he'd found at La Couarde, and have a swim before supper.

"I've had an idea about doing something completely different tomorrow."

With some reluctance, Frances agreed, "if it wouldn't take too long".

"Inside 15 minutes I'd say – it really isn't far to cycle."

When they were in the sea, she asked about his idea for the next day.

"I thought we could go and see historic La Rochelle. By bus!"

"What? By public transport, you mean?"

"Yes, we can drive to St Martin and leave the car. Then catch the bus which will take us over the bridge and land us right in the middle of La Rochelle. I mean, the bus fare'll be much less than the cost of the Bridge toll and cark park charges in the city if we went all the way by car. It'll be something different. What do you think?"

"Sounds like a great idea. My backside could do with a rest from that saddle!"

"Yes, and on that score, why don't we make the day afterwards a Rest Day with a minimum of cycling anywhere, and maybe make it a Beach Day?"

"You're on, Toby. I like it. Good plan." She gave him another of those smiles which was beginning to mean much more to him.

"Now, come on, let's do some swimming. I'm getting cold just listening to you! Er, no offence!"

"S'OK," he grinned. "I was thinking the same."

The next day was more cloudy but the temperature was otherwise pleasant enough. They caught the bus to La Rochelle from the town stop close to the harbour, and then had to put up with the fact that of course its route took them all round the houses and not straight to the Bridge. Still, they weren't in a rush and had plenty of time. They were due to reach the city by noon and felt that three or four hours spent nosing around would be plenty before catching the return service around tea-time.

Getting off at the city's bus station, they searched around for, and found, a plan of the centre of the city. Happily they were already not far from the famous fortified harbour and could go down that street over *there*, and then take *that* street off it, and so quickly come to the harbour. To Frances' delight, 'that street over *there*' turned out to be taking them past a lot of very expensive-looking shops, and of course Toby had to stand politely by while she gazed at all the bags and shoes and hats and dresses, and the rest! He was lucky to find that she knew her limitations and did not spend long actually *inside* any of the shops. He wisely held his tongue as she oohed over this and aahed at that, and he gave the right sort of non-committal grunt or nod if she asked his opinion. Not that *that* mattered, he knew. But he could see she was happy, and that counted for a lot.

At last they emerged at the harbour. Turning round, Toby mentally marked the way back to the bus station. Then they realised that they were overdue for something to eat and so looked for a suitable café. It was a relief to both of them that they agreed they couldn't possibly afford those restaurant prices! They tried a few side-streets where they came across a much cheaper menu, and so satisfied their hunger sufficiently to tide them over until supper time later on.

They spent the afternoon walking round the harbour and down onto the fortified walls. Both of them took plenty of photographs which, in Toby's case, included a number of Frances, surreptitiously taken to catch a natural moment here and there, as well as the posed shots. What he didn't realise was that Frances was doing the same thing when he wasn't looking. He found out when she showed them to him later that evening!

Partly as a result of sitting closely together on the bus both ways, and also because they had now had four days of being together all the time, they had become familiarly easy with each other. They spent the latter part of the evening after supper curled up cosily together, he with his book, she reading her Kindle. Once again it felt very companionable. He had his arm draped loosely round her shoulder but something was holding him back from anything more physical.

He was still suffering from uncertainties which he could no longer define. He saw she was like a valuable picture coming ever more into sharper focus, but he just couldn't shake off the old feelings resulting from all those earlier questions.

And what did she really feel about him? Was friendship all she wanted from him? He knew, if she had come on strong and been all over him like Claudia had done recently, he would have backed off immediately, and fast.

But Frances wasn't Claudia – far from it, and here she was, virtually in his arms, demanding nothing from him, and still he had doubts. What was he afraid of? What was there about her to be afraid of? Nothing of course, but even having that much certainty wasn't helping him. He cursed himself inwardly, but that didn't help things either. There was no-one waving a magic wand for *him*. And, in the end, he took refuge in doing nothing. Procrastination could be a useful temporary solution sometimes …..

Chapter Fourteen

And Finally …..

Love is the opening door;
Love is what we came here for.
No-one could offer you more.
Do you know what I mean?
(Elton John, 1970)

As they had agreed, Thursday was to be a day
for R&R. The only cycling that morning would
be down to the beach and back. The day was a
lot warmer, the sun out, one of those fine blue
September days. No need to rush. They took their
time getting their stuff ready for the beach – no
food, as it was easier to come back for lunch, and
better for them to do that if the day should turn
out to be summer-hot during the early afternoon.

They parked and locked up their bikes and walked
some distance along the beach, setting up camp
high up where the sand met the dunes. There were
still a few families and the odd couple on the same
stretch of beach, but all were well-spaced apart so
that Toby and Frances could almost feel private
where they were. Certainly there appeared to be

no risk of having to put up with someone else's noisy chatter, music, or a dog yapping.

The sun was not yet at its hottest, and the breeze across the beach was pleasantly slight, so they spread out their towels next to each other, stripped off down to their bathers, and settled down for a spot of sun-bathing. Or rather, in Toby's case, he got out a pen and a crossword and started to apply his mind. After he had tried a few clues, and almost without thinking, he started to throw the odd clue at Frances. He didn't stop to think that she might not be interested, and he didn't pick up on her initial lack of response. He accepted it as perfectly natural when, after a while of these intermittent interruptions, she gave a loud sigh, put down her Kindle and sat up beside him, leaning over close to see how far he'd got. Perhaps despite herself she couldn't help joining in.

"2 Down, it's 'Dwindle'. D for daughter, Le for the Frenchman, and Wind for the 'Hot air inside'. See? And 10 Across, 4 letters, is 'Iris' – you know, another word for Flag as well as an Eye, both of which are part of the clue."

"Thanks," he said, and wrote the two answers in. After that, they worked at the crossword together and completed most of it before Frances lay back again and returned to her Kindle. Toby picked up his book, lay on his back and started reading. And began to doze off in the warmth of the sun.

After a while, something woke him up – what, he didn't know, and he turned over to see if Frances was still reading. She seemed to be asleep, lying there looking so relaxed and peaceful. Her Kindle lay on the edge of her towel where her unconscious hand had let it fall. He raised himself up on his elbow and gazed at her, sorting out his thoughts.

He had to admit that she looked pretty good in that bikini. Nothing skimpy, and everywhere was covered or contained that needed to be. Definitely a nice shape, and not anything like the thin scrawny figure of a girl he remembered from Junior School. Her shoulder-length hair was tied back, but loosely, so that it still spilled over on one side. He continued to think. And to gaze. And then to realise a significant truth: that he had always been comfortable with her ever since they had met again in Normandy.

All of a sudden, it hit him, as clear as day. As if all his uncertainties had evaporated under the sun's warmth. It was all so blindingly obvious; how could he not have seen it before? Or perhaps he always had done but could never admit it. What did that matter now? He knew. He just knew. Completely. And there she was. She said she had wanted to be with *him*, *he* had been her choice, and there she was lying right beside him! He gulped. It had to be *now*. This couldn't wait a moment longer. He bent over and kissed her lips as lightly as he could, hoping not to wake her.

She opened one eye and raised an eyebrow at him. She had not been asleep.

"Toby Stannard! What do you call *that*? Do it again, d'you hear? And this time, jolly well do it properly!"

Momentarily taken aback by the sharpness of her response, which made him feel like a naughty schoolboy caught in the act, he did as he was told. He kissed her again, with purpose, concentrating solely on the feel of her lips under his; they were firm but unresisting. This set a delicious sensation falling through him down to the depths of his stomach.

As he left off, she said gently:

"For goodness sake - and about time too! What on earth kept you?" She looked him full in the eyes and smiled. "Now it's my turn," she murmured.

She reached up and curled her arms around his neck and drew his mouth down to meet hers. Her kiss was as deep as the one she had given him in her flat that evening on his birthday.

The world around him disappeared: the beach, the sea, the people. All he knew for several glorious seconds was the fact of her kiss, the pressure of her lips on his, and the warm snugness of her arms as she held him to her. In truth it was only seconds, but for him that kiss seemed to last an hour. When she drew back, he felt as if he had just lost a diamond.

"There," she said softly. "Isn't that better?

He nodded dumbly but with the broadest grin on his face.

"And don't you think it's time we did a lot more of it, you and me? We've waited long enough. I'm pretty sure you have, haven't you? I've watched you." She chuckled. "And I know I have," she added, "quite long enough."

His eyes came back into focus properly, and the delicate smell of her filled his nostrils. He couldn't stop grinning. Foolishly, but happily. He couldn't take his eyes off hers as she held him in her steady gaze.

"Phew, Ro, that was just incredible. Completely and utterly terrific!"

In the magic of the moment, he didn't notice that he had used – and shortened – her first name. So he wasn't aware that she *didn't* react to it, didn't even blink, where once she would have hit the roof.

"My innards are putty, my knees are probably jelly by now, and I'm feeling as light as air. This isn't supposed to happen to blokes, is it?"

He paused.

"And, best of all, you've just given me the answer I've been trying to find for ages. God, how incredibly blind I've been!"

"Toby Stannard, are you sure you weren't born on a Thursday?"

He suddenly looked blank; the reference was lost on him.

"I mean," she said, "You've taken so long to get here. How come you've been so slow to realise what was right under your nose, what was happening between us?"

"I suppose I couldn't see the wood for the trees. All I could see were uncertainties, and nothing ever cleared until that moment as I lay looking at you a little while ago – I thought you were asleep. And suddenly, out of nowhere, it all clicked, all made sense. Next thing, your kiss confirmed what I should have twigged on my birthday. Doesn't that seem so long ago now!"

"Don't worry, I'm not mad at you. I'm just so glad you got here at long last – and I'm relieved. I was getting fed up with waiting for you to make the first move. Wasn't I giving you clear enough signs?"

"Sorry, just couldn't read them, obviously."

She sighed.

"I guess that's men for you! But look, we've now proved I was right not to give up on you, and now you've got over the line. I've got you in my camp at last, so now I can cross over into yours."

She paused.

"And thank you, Toby, for being one of the very few people who saw me as I am and not what I tried to be. And for sticking by me when you must have thought I had turned into someone else."

"My pleasure," he replied. "And the most important thing is: I got there in the end, didn't I? And it really is brilliant!"

"Of course it is, it's meant to be like that. At least, I've always thought so. So was it the kiss that made the difference?"

"Not entirely, no. There's the realisation, of course. But it's this feeling of complete certainty that's the best part. And that's all down to you. Now, come here and let's do it all over again. I want to see if we can improve on the previous effort!"

He put his arms round her back and shoulders and pulled her closer to him. He felt the warmth of her tummy on his. And then lower down.

"Hmm, somebody seems pleased to see me!" she grinned.

He had of course been properly hard ever since she kissed him, but it was the feel of her closeness which set the little chap straining upwards even more strongly.

Which she felt against her own body. She eased off slightly, and slid her hand down inside his shorts, coming to rest with her fingers holding his erect penis.

"Didn't I do this once before, I think? And he's even more anxious to see me now, isn't he?" She almost crooned the words.

"Careful, careful!" warned Toby but this time he made no move to dissuade her.

"Has he ever heard of the lady who lived deep in the dark woods?" she asked. "Or was it a warm cave? I forget." Her voice all at once dreamy, she wasn't really speaking to him now – more to the chap in her hand. "Would he like to pay a visit?

Come and say hello soon?"

Toby gently pulled her chin upwards so that he could talk to her face and not her hair. "Ro, for the second time you've caught me unequipped for what you're talking about. You can tell that he'd love to, but if he's screaming Yes, my head is trying to hold on to control and say Not here, Not now. And not without insurance. You know what I mean, of course!"

"Yes, I do, and I also know that in France you can buy them easily over the counter in supermarkets or chemists."

"Well, I haven't got any."

"And your point is? So what's your problem? Just jolly well go and get some! No, not now, silly. Later. On the way home, we can see if Mr Carrefour can help, if the Pharmacie isn't still open."

"Meanwhile ……," he said.

"Meanwhile, I'm taking my hand away gently, see? We don't want any spillages, do we? I suggest a swim right now, to cool off a little."

"Oh yes, definitely!" said Toby, much relieved.

"But first, two things," she said. "Firstly, come here and give me another nice kiss."

They held each other close again. "And second?" he asked.

"Secondly, I need your hand for a moment."

Obediently he surrendered his right hand. Immediately she slipped it inside her own bikini bottoms and drew his fingers down her smooth tummy and on into the velvet of her own warm silk-soft hair. She held his hand there for a few moments.

"That feels nice," she murmured. "And now you have been introduced." She drew his hand gently out again. And curled her own fingers around his. "The social niceties should be observed, don't you agree? It's a two-way relationship, you know. I like to think it'll bring us together more completely." She smiled at him.

"And the bathe?" he asked.

"Yep, I'm ready. Let's do it."

Hand-in-hand they walked into the water. Where there was a lot more cuddling than swimming.

And hand-in-hand they walked back up the beach to towel down.

"Let's go out somewhere this evening," Toby said suddenly. "To eat, I mean."

"Lovely idea! Did you have anywhere particular in mind?"

"Goodness! Around here the world's our oyster – so many restaurants to choose from. Stacks of them in St Martin by the harbour, and there are quite a few in La Flotte on the promenade and around the harbour there. More probably in La Couarde too. And in the village of course. A lot of them look pretty pricey. There's even one just round the corner which looks nice. The thing is, I know it's almost the end of the holiday, but I don't want to blow the last of my money just to push food down my throat. So I'd vote for a more reasonably-priced one."

"Well, you know I've got even less spare than you have, so I'm definitely with you on that one. So where to go?"

"OK, let's decide it this way. How far do you want to go? If you want to stay local, let's do the one a few roads away. If you want to get out of the village, let's drive up to St Martin and walk down to the harbour. We'd have the best choice of menu prices there, and I'll bet the evening atmosphere can be quite nice."

"Oh come on. Let's do the second. Let's find a nice medium-priced restaurant in St Martin." She gave him a hug. "You and your good ideas!"

"Meanwhile, let's get back for some lunch. We can then decide whether we want to come back down to the beach this afternoon or go somewhere else."

"Or not go somewhere else?" she suggested mischievously.

"Down boy!" Toby said firmly. "Let's wait and see later what we feel like doing."

The weather was still fine after lunch, and Rowena/Frances still complained about having sore nethers from the cycling, so more of that was vetoed.

"If we're driving out this evening, let's go back down to the beach now, while it's still lovely and warm. I hadn't finished sunbathing when you attacked me without provocation, *if* you remember!" She accused him with mock indignation. "Let alone finishing my book! And you'll have to learn to keep your hands off me if I'm to get any peace and quiet!"

"*Really*?" He could see she was teasing.

"Really really! No, of course not, you clot! Don't be a fathead! Why would I want you to keep your distance when I've only recently just about thrown myself at you?"

"Idiot!" he said, giving her another hug.

"Idiot back!" came the instant reply, together with another of her amazing kisses.

They didn't hurry to get themselves ready for the beach. Kiss was followed by counter-kiss, hug by counter-hug.

"Oh come on! This isn't getting us anywhere!" she laughed.

"What do you mean?" he replied indignantly. "Of course it is. We're just getting more acquainted, that's all. That's very important when you've just found the right girl!"

"Yes, OK, you're right. But, come on, Toby, or we'll miss the sunshine. Can we drive down to the beach this time? It'll be quicker and I want to make the most of it."

And so they returned to the beach and to the same spot as before. *Their* spot, they were both calling it already. And for the rest of the afternoon they lay and soaked up the sun, had a couple of quick dips in the sea, dried each other off; and Toby left her alone – more or less – to finish the story on her Kindle. He polished off another crossword, largely without her help. Otherwise he snoozed – he was still feeling euphoric from the morning's explosion and wanted it to last for as long as he could hang onto the sensation.

They returned to shower off and change, and played the game of trying to avoid touching each other for at least 5 minutes. A good game when you only have a confined space to move around in and are positively looking for ways to lose! The game ended when one of them ended up clutching a wine bottle and two glasses.

"Come on, let's just sit quietly outside and enjoy the growing dusk with a glass of Rosé."

"OK, you win. And the game?"

"I lost more times than you did, so really don't I win?"

"Who cares? Come and have some wine."

In due course it was time to get in the car and drive up to St Martin.

"Don't forget to go round by the centre of the village, Toby" said R/F.

"Why?"

"Remember, you need to see the man in Carrefour about getting some hats!"

"Ah, got you!," he twigged her euphemism.

"Let's hope he's still got some!"

A few minutes later, he emerged from the little supermarket beaming and patting his pocket.

"All set!" he told her as he got in the car.

She gave him a radiant smile in return, squeezed his arm affectionately, and let him drive her up to the town. He parked in the pétanque square behind the church and they walked down to the quayside. Even though it was September and the French national holidays were over, there were still a fair few restaurants open. They walked up past each one, scrutinising every menu, and then back. In the end they retraced their steps and chose the last one in the row. No trouble finding a table for two. They ordered.

"So tomorrow's our last day here." Toby sat holding her hand across the table. "What would you like to do? You choose; I've done all the other days."

"Please can we come and look round St Martin properly?"

"You mean more shops?"

"What do *you* think? Of course! What else would a girl want to do? But there's the market too. And the harbour to walk round properly. And the battlements."

"Yes, and the church. I want to show you that too. And did you know you can go up the tower? We've definitely got to do that – you get fantastic views from up there, and I can reuse my ticket from the last time. Got to be a winner!" he said enthusiastically.

"So that's settled. I get the shops and you get to speak only when I ask your opinion! No, it's OK, I'm only joking. From now on, your opinion's going to matter to me a lot more. As I hope mine will be to you," she said, looking at him meaningfully.

"It's alright, I get the message," he grinned. "It goes with the territory. Of respecting each other, I mean. I wouldn't think much of me if I didn't do that. Just so long as you'll remember to be kind when you bring it to my attention if I forget."

"So don't forget. Or at least try not to," she softened, and smiled to show that she wasn't laying down the law at him.

"Anything or anywhere else tomorrow?"

"Well, I think we should have one last bike ride but not a long one. Don't we have to return them by the end of the afternoon?"

"Yes we do. Thanks for reminding me."

"So, I'd like to cycle along the top path past those oyster beds we saw on my first ride. Let's do that circuit, coming straight back down to La Couarde and home across the fields."

"OK. And after we've taken the bikes back?"

"We do our packing, clean the place up ready for leaving in the morning, and then go out to that local restaurant you told me about. We could walk there, or drive – you said it's not all that far."

"Fine. We can ride by there and book a table for the evening, on our way up to St Martin in the morning."

"Aren't we driving?"

"Well, we could do, but I feel we ought to get the most out of our bikes while we've got them. After all, they cost enough to hire. But only," he added, "if it's not going to make you more uncomfortable."

"I see what you mean about getting our money's worth. And I can always pad up. It's never as far as you think it's going to be so, yes OK, we'll cycle to St Martin in the morning.

The food arrived. They tucked in. Suddenly he chuckled to himself.

"What?" she asked, intrigued.

"Oh, nothing really. I was just thinking about Claude and how she was all over me that time in the pub. Like she was trying to gobble me up! I still don't really get it."

"Do you mind, the way things have turned out?" she said, teasing him.

"Phew! Not me! Maybe she was just having some fun at my expense. Does she like watching blokes squirm?"

"I told you before: Claude's OK. No, she's not malicious. I think she saw the way you looked at me, even if you weren't aware you were doing it. She admitted to me later that she thought she'd have some fun trying to buck you up!"

"Huh! Didn't work, though, did it?"

"No it didn't. I remember looking on, half-amused by her performance and your reaction. A bit of me was jealous about you; as far as I was concerned, you were mine to claim even then. And another bit of me was afraid you'd actually fall for it and go with her. Then I'd end up envying her for it. I was so glad by the end of the evening that you couldn't wait to get away from her – talk about a scared rabbit! And here I am, very happy that I've got you at last."

She suddenly became embarrassed, thinking she might have said the wrong thing at that moment. She couldn't afford for him to think it had all been just a case of her getting her own claws into him. She bent her head and attended to her meal.

"So, that apart, and on a completely different subject," Toby continued after a while of nothing but eating, "do I have permission to return to the fold tonight? After all, it *is* my bedroom. Technically. Even though I did surrender it willingly to you."

"You'll be in trouble, Toby Stannard, if you don't!" replied R/F hotly. "I haven't come all this way to find you, only to have to sleep alone the whole time." Her tone immediately softened. "You do want to, don't you?"

"Don't worry. If you're sure that's what *you* really want, then I'm your man." And let no man put us asunder, he thought. "You found me, and now, wonderfully, I've found you. Properly found you. And you clearly trust me or you wouldn't ask. I think you probably couldn't pay me a greater compliment."

He paused and thought for a moment.

"Actually," he began again, "I'm not sure if there's a greater honour a man can be given, I mean, when a girl offers herself freely. After all, it *is* a gift, isn't it, an incredibly special one? Shouldn't it be like that, you know, each time? Certainly I'd like to be worthy of it, that is, with your help. That's how I see it, anyway."

He finished lamely, and then suddenly pulled a face.

"Oh God, sorry, sorry! That last bit must have sounded awful - so pompous. I really didn't mean it to come out that way. I just couldn't think how to say what I really meant."

"It's alright," she said gently, squeezing his hand. "Thank you for the compliment; that was nice. Look, I know exactly what you're trying to say, and I think it confirms what I know about you, and why I've come to trust you so completely over these last twelve months." These past twenty years, more like, she said to herself.

She voiced some of her thoughts.

"Funny how a child of only 8 or 9 can prove to be so trustworthy, and yet neither he nor anyone else around him at that age has any idea of what that means. You have to be a grown adult to appreciate it."

She gave him a serious look and held his hand again.

"And, Toby Stannard, I do appreciate you."

He smiled at the compliment from her this time. Then gave her a curious look.

"Ro, what are you, some sort of white witch?"

She raised an eyebrow at that. "Meaning?" she asked suspiciously.

"Well, it's like you could've waved a wand over me, or something, and whatever else you may have done, you've opened my eyes and cleared my head of all those nagging doubts. Look at me - I'm so much happier for it, and I want to thank you. Life feels better already. If you can bear to stick around long enough, we can keep it going, yes? I mean, together, Ro."

She nodded, returning his smile affectionately.

Talking stopped while they carried on eating.

"Toby, you're calling me 'Ro' now. Where did that suddenly spring from? Not that I mind," she added hastily, "but normally I'd have come down on you – or anyone else for that matter – like a ton of hot bricks. You'd have done *that* only once! But suddenly, coming from you, I find I like it. It feels nicely intimate somehow."

"Do you remember, I told you when we first re-met and I discovered that you were you, that I've always liked the name Rowena. Unusual I know, but there it is. But this morning, it just came out that way: "Ro"; it was such a tender moment and it just seemed the right thing to say. But of course I'll stop straightaway if you say so."

"No. Let it stay. But just between us. Let's keep the intimacy. It's ours but it's private. Yes?"

"Agreed. And thank you for not laughing at me or slinging it back in my face. I'm not used to 'tender moments' but with you they're something special and I'd like a lot more of them. Please. And that's not a request."

He paused.

"Now, hurry up with that plate. I've finished mine and I want my dessert! And then we'll have coffee. Or do you want to go home for coffee?"

She reached across and took his hand again.

"That sounds so nice when you say it like that: "go home for coffee". Yes, I'd like to go "home" with you, Toby Stannard. So after dessert, let's get the bill and do exactly that, for coffee."

When they got back to the car, before starting off, Toby glanced across at her, expecting to exchange a smile. Instead he was alarmed to see her sitting staring ahead and looking worried all of a sudden.

"What's the matter, Ro?"

He reached across and, awkwardly, tried to give her a hug. She pushed him away.

"No, Toby, let me alone for a minute, will you? I need to be serious."

"What's wrong, Ro?" he asked gently.

"I was just thinking. I admit it's really great the way things have turned out. But, Toby, what do you really think of me? No, don't look like that at me – I need you to be truthful. Do you *really* want me? Because ….." she gulped nervously, "because, you know, I'm spoiled goods now. Some might even say "damaged goods" though I think that'd be going a bit too far. I told you what happened, and it's all true. So do you think of me as second-hand? I can tell you're obviously still excited about us after this morning on the beach. But I keep thinking about that song: "Will You Still Love Me Tomorrow?" You know what I mean: tomorrow, or the next day, or maybe the next, or even the next month, when you start seeing things differently because you've had time to think about it."

She looked pained at the thought.

"I'm sorry, Toby. I was just thinking ……..", and her voice trailed off uncertainly.

Toby's initial reaction to this speech found him almost incredulous. He sat there momentarily lost for words. Then he began to see it from her point of view. That lack of self-confidence suddenly showing its ugly self again. He thought quickly: do *not* scoff at her fears. He took a deep breath.

"I'm OK with it, really I am, Ro" he said as tenderly as he could.

"Alright, so I admit I'd like to meet that bloke and punch his effing lights out! Every single one of them. For good! And I'd like someone – or something – to do to him what he did to you, pain and all!"

His moment of anger passed quickly.

"But, Ro, I want you as you are. I mean, I would like you to be with me as you are, not as you might have been, or in any other way. And I don't mean 'warts and all' either. I don't see you like that. I've always tried to see the person inside you, although I admit I like what's on the outside too!"

She smiled at that.

"And it's the Rowena Frances inside I want to learn more about. OK, so you've had a frightening experience, but you've already come beyond that and I'd like to think it's finally in the past for you. What can I say? That part's up to you to deal with, but I'll help you all I can, if you'll let me. And give me enough time. Look, when I see you, I want to touch you, to hold you. When I hold you close, I get this marvellous warm desire to enfold you and, especially after what happened to you, to shield you. You know, show you the respect you deserve. I don't mean 'to look after you' – that's romantic tosh and anyway it's patronising. You don't need that. But it's lovely to feel that I'm holding you safe. I don't know if that's love or not, but I can tell you it's all because of you. So, yes, I do really want you, since you ask!"

She seemed satisfied with his reply and gave him a grateful smile.

"Sorry. I suddenly saw myself losing you. But it's alright, I feel better now. Thank you."

"OK to go now?"

"Yes," she said. "Let's go home."

*　　*　　*　　*　　*

As to the rest of the evening, suffice to say that it's not all that easy for either party to drink their coffee when they're wrapped around each other in a cosy armchair – and a small one at that. And after? After they had gone outside to gaze at the stars, they were at last lying together in each other's arms in a comfortable bed, sometimes still, sometimes stroking hair, cheek, body, and kissing anything and everything that got in the way. And in a while and a while they rolled over and knew the next move would take them over the line. He broke away from her embrace briefly to put on the necessary, then came back to her and gently slipped inside her. She stretched up, luxuriating in the tenderness of his touch, inside her and outside. Her arms came back down and round his neck, to clasp him in love and hold him to her, showing him that she was his for the asking.

Marvellously, he felt he had all the time in the world. No need to hurry. Keep the latent passion under control and just focus on the tenderness. Caressing her breasts, hips and thighs with his fingertips, he moved slowly inside her, in and back, further in and back. He saw this graceful swimmer in his mind's eye and thought: Yes, be graceful in your movement; she who is graceful deserves it. Give her the love she deserves. And missed the first time. Never mind this delicious body: look deep into her eyes, see the real girl you're making love with. Feel it and know how she is touching your soul as much as your body. And a flush of love for the girl came surging through his being.

Each gave to the other, and received back in kind, in gentle passion and its delicious electricity.

And there came a point where, instead of relaxing under his smooth rhythmic movement, she tightened her grip on him. All around. At the same moment he felt her warm moist tongue delve into his ear, its movement an extra encouragement to spur him on. She thrust herself against him. His senses exploded even as he felt the urgency of her inside as well as outside her, and knew it was her way of asking him to come, that she was ready for him to step up the tempo and power forward strongly to the end, to the Golden Moment and into temporary oblivion.

It was immediate, it was a release, a unifying act. She clasped him tightly to her body, and with surprising strength. In that moment she flooded his total consciousness, his entire being. Absolutely nothing but her mattered to him. He clung to her, trying to sink into her softness, with no thought but to make the moment last for as long as possible.

How long can 'possible' be? Not long enough for either of them. But then they had the afterglow too. They lay entwined, as one, a perfect fit. For a while it was as if they were sharing the same space in the cosmos. In his head Toby heard the voice of Graham Nash singing: "I never want to finish what I've just begun with you."

And finally, one word. The same word from each mind, one a question, one an affirmation.

"Home?" she said softly.

"Home." he breathed.

And added, "At last".

They'd made it. Arrived. Finally.

*   *   *   *   *

And the end of the story? On their last day on the island, they did everything they'd planned. On the day of departure, they set off in good time and headed back the way they'd come. He handed over control of the iPod to her – her choice to play or ignore. They stopped for lunch beneath the fairy-tale castle the girls had spotted on the journey down. They made time to have a short stroll around the little town which sat before the castle's imposing front gates.

The overnight stop was in a quaint old 15th century manor house in the middle of rolling countryside. They missed the right turning and found themselves driving down a field track to reach the place – Google maps not giving the most accurate of directions! But the proprietor was charming, and had some excellent cider to offer them.

On the way back to Calais and the Tunnel, they enjoyed passing views, places, landmarks which had been spotted on the way down two weeks earlier. They didn't stop in Rouen but spent some pleasant minutes remembering the coach tour, the people on it, and the things that happened, particularly between themselves. She told him all about her trip to the Dordogne, the chambres d'hôtes they had stayed in, and what she had especially enjoyed. They both agreed that a visit together sometime in the future would be worth it.

And so, a fair few hours later, they finally arrived back in Balham. Toby lugged her case and bags upstairs to the flat where they found Jane watching TV. She saw immediately that things had changed between them and she hugged them both. "Welcome back, and I'm really happy for the two of you!"

They thanked her but, because Toby was parked on a yellow line and it was late and they had, after all, had a long drive, he decided to take his leave there and then, refusing the offer of a cup of coffee.

He and Rowena Frances said goodbye downstairs in the front hall. And kissed goodbye again. And then again.

"See you again very soon?" she pleaded.

"Oh, you bet!" he replied, giving her another huge hug. "I'm not letting you get away twice, now that you've chosen me!"

"That makes two of us, remember? You've chosen me too. OK, I'll give you a bell tomorrow when I get in from work. Unless you can't wait and you want to do lunch?"

"Always a pleasure, never a chore," he laughed. He kissed her once more, left, and she waved him off, returning to the flat upstairs where Jane was eagerly waiting to hear all about the holiday.

THE END

About the Author

R Mark Ellis Brown was born in Leicester early in January 1951. Both his parents came from two musical families, one professional and one amateur; with his two  older brothers he was educated at Wells Cathedral School where he became joint head boy in the school choir. Music and singing thereafter have dominated his life. At college in Guildford, he gained his diploma in Business Studies in 1971. In 1973 he joined the Royal Academy of Music as their Assistant Accountant. He married in 1978 and has two children. From accounting he moved in time into software systems training and business analysis for 21 years until redundancy due to the 2008 financial crash. Until retirement in 2016 he was the Accountant's Assistant at St Catherine's School Bramley.

He lives in a pleasant village near Guildford with his wife; they are both members of the church choir at St Mary's, Frensham, near Farnham. His interests include steam trains, tennis, writing, his four grandchildren, jig-saw puzzles, Liverpool & Leicester City football teams, and holidays in SW France.

Other titles by the author include:

Trust in Strangers

The Misunderstanding

A Question of Guilt

A Light That Failed

Moments of Grace

Fridays – Four Better, Four Worse

book design by

Printed in Poland
by Amazon Fulfillment
Poland Sp. z o.o., Wrocław

60952612R00166